# Discovering the
# *Soul*
## of Your Story

---

*Second Edition*

## Roger Rueff

Published by Transcend Press
Chicago, Illinois

Copyright 2015 by Roger Rueff
Second Edition
ISBN 978-0-9844688-3-6 (Softcover)
ISBN 978-0-9844688-4-3 (Kindle e-reader)

*Discovering the Soul of Your Story*, First Edition - Copyright 2012

To join in the ongoing development and application of the principles and practices described in this book, visit the *Soul of Your Story Academy* website at:

www.soulofyourstory.com

For a description of the website and its features, see "Appendix A: Soul of Your Story Academy."

*To Jennifer Rueff, whose love and support have made this undertaking possible. And to Dylan Rueff, for his helpful creativity—and also just for being a terrific son.*

# ACKNOWLEDGMENTS

My gratitude for help in producing this work flows in many directions, most of which point toward the students I have been fortunate enough to instruct in my classes at Chicago Dramatists and the Northwestern University Summer Writers' Conference. Either I have lived an extraordinarily righteous life and have been rewarded by the Teaching Gods with a consistent stream of bright and interested students or the subject matter has hit a common nerve among smart writers and attracted those who are ready to absorb it. In either case, I have undergone an almost-uninterrupted zapping with the lucky stick, and it is largely through my students' quests to understand the principles I present in this book that I have been prompted to hone and refine those principles, so that they are both potent and easy to learn.

Above all, though, I am grateful to my two intrepid reviewers, Keri Ellis and David Lee, who have slogged through the mire of my drafts with intelligent grace and demonstrated extraordinary patience and insight in the process. With each new draft, I have composed for their benefit a tongue-in-cheek personalized acknowledgment to amuse them, but for publication I will resort to sincerity and say simply that I appreciate their efforts more than I can express, and I will be forever grateful to them.

They're brilliant people and wonderful friends, and they deserve for the world to know it.

# CONVENTIONS USED IN THIS BOOK

This book employs certain conventions with regard to its use of italics and gender references. You would pick up on them pretty quickly just by reading, but it seldom hurts to spell things out when one can.

## ITALICS

Throughout this book, I italicize words and phrases that comprise key elements or matters of concern regarding its fundamental topics, not merely upon first appearance but wherever they are referenced. The purpose of this convention is to provide the reader with immediate visual cues regarding words or phrases that are of particular importance to the subject matter.

I also italicize story titles and scientific references, where appropriate. And from time to time I do use italics for emphasis—but *very* rarely.

## GENDER REFERENCES

Because the principles presented in this book apply equally well to writers of both genders, it is important that its language reflect gender-neutrality without muddling the text or confusing the reader. To do so without resorting to awkward forms such as "he or she," "he/she," "(s)he," "s/he," or "zhe," I employ the following conventions.

- In Part One, the writer, audience member, and person on the street are referred to using the masculine gender, and the feminine gender is reserved for story characters of non-specific gender.
- In Part Two and Part Three, the convention of Part One is reversed.

Given the page count, that renders things pretty much equal as far as the language is concerned.

# TABLE OF CONTENTS

## Part Three — Meta-adaptation

## Appendices

# PREFACE TO THE SECOND EDITION

In the two and a half years since I first published this book, I have been heartened and delighted by the responses that I have received from writers around the country who have greatly appreciated its new approach to thinking about stories. Many of those writers tell me that they have taken a slew of creative writing courses, none of which has provided them with the clear and comprehensive view of storytelling that this book does. And some of them have gone on to explore that view further, especially as it relates to their own works-in-progress, by taking the online course that I offer on the support site for the book, www.soulofyourstory.com.

It has also become clear to me, however, that some readers have struggled with certain bits of nomenclature that I used in the first edition, simply because the words or phrases came across as too technical. The two that have been most problematic are *"vector of intent"* and *"condition of value"*—both of which are fundamental to the concepts described in the book.

So I gave a lot of thought to alternative phrasing, with an eye toward retaining the original meaning while making it easier to understand. And the alternative phrasing that best fits the bill is this:

- *"vector of intent"* becomes *"type of intent"*
- *"condition of value"* becomes *"treasure"*

Because of my engineering background, I have a very clear concept of what a *vector* is, but most people do not. And the subtleties of its definition, such as magnitude and direction, are simply not necessary to the idea that it is meant to convey. So *"type"* is a fine replacement.

Likewise, although *"condition of value"* accurately represents the concept to which it applies, it is not a term that one encounters in everyday life. The term *"treasure,"* on the other hand, bears a universal meaning that is easy to understand and expresses the same idea.

So that's what we're going with.

Other than that, not much has changed in this version of the book aside from a simplification of the statements that define the three *types of intent*. In fact, if the two phrases I addressed above were not so fundamental to the concepts in the book, and so pervasive in its text, it would not have been necessary to designate this version as a second edition; I could have simply tweaked and republished the original.

But they are, and it is.

So here you have it.

# PREFACE TO THE FIRST EDITION

I have written this book to reveal to anyone who might be intrigued by its title the details of a set of story creation and development techniques I have invented and named "the *grok approach*," "*thematic imprinting*," and "*meta-adaptation*."

The *grok approach* helps the writer explore the motivations of his characters and their impacts on the plot and action. *Thematic imprinting* makes use of a unique new grammar for expressing the *theme* of a story and works hand-in-hand with the *grok approach* to convey that *theme* through the plot and *outcome*. *Meta-adaptation* combines the two techniques into an overall practice that the writer can use to generate stories from the most basic of ideas using a wide array of starting points.

I developed these techniques for one reason only—to satisfy a personal desire to understand storytelling on a level deeper than I was able to attain by taking classes or reading books on the subject. I have, in fact, read a fair number of books about storytelling, and some of them are excellent. Those that are not so excellent typically provide little more than a broad-brush treatment, regurgitating tired old principles that have passed through so many hands that they are now threadbare and missing their stuffing. Some brim with exercises that may serve as useful practice for certain storytelling tasks but do not comprise a unified approach to storytelling or speak to its grander issues. Others are short on exercises but filled with vague counsel that amounts to little more than soft advice on how to tell a story.

I did not want soft advice; I wanted hard advice—advice that I could reach for confidently to generate new stories from scratch, guide their development, and fix any problems that might arise along the way. But none of the books I had read, nor any class or workshop I had ever attended, was able to satisfy my desire to know a story deeply, and by "deeply" I mean at the level of its soul—the ineffable thing that binds its pieces together, speaks to its audience on a subconscious level, holds the attention of that audience organically, and rewards it with insight, amusement, and a strong, internal movement of the spirit.

What I wanted was a reliable "something" that, as far as I could tell, did not exist.

So I created it.

# Part One

## The *grok* Approach

---

# Chapter 1

## First Principles

In addition to my creative writing achievements, I possess an advanced degree in engineering. And like every other trained engineer who has ever walked the Earth, I was taught early on in my education to look to "first principles" when trying to understand any natural process. To claim a complete understanding of a process, one must be able to derive its workings from the basic physics that govern its operations. It is not enough to know how to use a time-tested equation; a competent engineer should also know the underpinnings of the equation and be able to reproduce it by starting with the simplest aspects of the problem, applying the appropriate physics, and recreating the equation from scratch. To do so requires a command and veneration of first principles.

The reason that engineering students are taught how to derive important equations, rather than simply applying them by rote, is that the knowledge of how to use the equations is often less important than is the ability to recreate them from whole cloth. An equation may apply to a given situation, but the knowledge of how it was derived equips the engineer to invent new equations, as necessary—to make something fresh from that bolt of whole cloth and solve new problems as they arise.

The challenge for me at the outset of this quest to develop a new approach to storytelling was that, unlike engineering, the building blocks of storytelling are not measurable elements of the physical world like molecular weights or vapor pressures. The building blocks of storytelling lie not in the realm of Nature per se, but in the minds and hearts of the audience. And although modern scanning techniques can reveal which parts of the brain spring to life when we experience certain emotions, that knowledge does nothing to advance our understanding of what makes a good story work. The brain is not the mind. The mind is not the heart. And the heart seems nearly unknowable.

Nearly.

For although no two people are completely alike, our psyches do not develop in a vacuum. Rather, each is formed in the same genetic mold that has pressed into shape its billions of global neighbors. It is not an exaggeration to say that a well-told story can produce roughly the same effect across wide swaths of cultural spectra as long as it speaks to the universals of being human. In this respect, we are each governed by the processes that formed our species and brought it to this point in its history. Whether you ascribe those forces to an omnipotent personal deity or chalk them up to the natural tendency of matter and energy to create intelligent life if the conditions are right, we arrive at the same conclusion—that you and I share a myriad of common feelings, perceptions, and ways of receiving and parsing information... as well as dreams, desires, and expectations.

And therein lies the basic hope for deriving a storytelling approach from first principles—the fact that the audience is human.

When I looked to the literature, however, there seemed to be few efforts to do so. What exists in most storytelling guides, with a few notable exceptions, is more of a hodgepodge of advice, admonition, and example than it is a unified practice that one can readily apply to any storytelling endeavor.

So I set myself to the task of building from the ground up something that, as far as I could tell, did not exist—a straightforward, self-consistent approach to storytelling. Something fresh, derived from basic ingredients, and full of potential, like an acorn. Something easy-to-use and brimming with implications that would reveal themselves to the writer in an unfolding manner over time and with repeated application and success. Something that he could use to cut away the tangled underbrush of possibilities that can grow up and threaten to overwhelm a developing story. Something that would help him to see the story clearly, all the way to its bones and bloodstream—to hear its heart beating and know how to shape it so that it matures to see a satisfying end.

Without knowing it at the time, I had given conceptual birth to the techniques I describe in this book—the *grok approach, thematic imprinting*, and *meta-adaptation*. All three can be used at any stage in the writing process: in the fertile "Hmmm..." stage where story ideas are spawned; in the sometimes-chaotic midst of story development, to solve problems as they arise or redirect a story that has gotten wildly off-track in the telling; and in the editing process, after the first draft is finished and the time comes to trim and hone. And they apply wherever the writer is on his path. Beginning writers find them useful, because they demystify the story creation process. Intermediate writers appreciate their ability to clear away the crust of inhibiting nonsense that tends to form around stories as they develop. And advanced writers welcome their tendency to unsettle old habits of thinking while reinforcing the notion that great stories are born from the spontaneous eruption of creative thought.

And so we begin the journey to reveal and apply them. And we do so exactly where all great story creation begins.

With the *main character*.

# Chapter 2

## THE MAIN CHARACTER

### RELATIONSHIP OF CHARACTER TO PLOT

Plot springs from character, not the other way around. Events by themselves do not make a story, regardless of their seeming magnitude. Impact requires importance, and no event can be judged important except in relation to the characters whom it might affect.

A massive plug of magma blasting through the crust of our planet four billion years ago might have presented a dazzling display if anyone had been here to see it, but it was not important in a storytelling sense, because nothing was alive to be influenced by its effects. An identical plug bursting from a volcano near a major modern city would be both spectacular and potentially devastating to inhabitants of the city. Same eruption, different day—one having no particular consequence except to the formation of what would someday become real estate, the other causing widespread destruction and tearing apart human lives in the process.

Stories require characters, not merely to populate and steer them but to drive them and imbue them with significance.

An airplane touching down on an airstrip in Morocco is not a story. A dashing freedom fighter and his beautiful wife walking into a nightclub owned by an American with whom the wife was once involved is not a story. An embittered nightclub owner grappling with memories of a happier past and working to maintain an emotional distance above and outside the fray of a war-torn world—and ultimately re-entering that world by performing a selfless act... *is* a story.

A young man in workout sweats punching a side of beef in a meat locker is not a story. That same young man dressed in boxing attire kneeling in prayer before the fight of his life is not a story. A young man with a mixed-results small-time boxing record accepting the seemingly impossible challenge of fighting the world heavyweight champion and setting his sights on performing a feat that no other boxer has been able to accomplish—to last the entire 15 rounds of the fight—in order to earn a sense of self-respect that he has never felt... *is* a story.

A train slamming into a bus filled with convicts on their way to a federal prison is not a story. A shackled convict jumping to safety and stumbling off into the countryside is not a story. A respected surgeon wrongly convicted of murdering his wife seizing the opportunity of a train/prison-bus crash to escape captivity and go in pursuit of the truth behind his wife's murder so that he can clear his name and bring the true perpetrator to justice... *is* a story.

Stories grow out of the decisions and actions that their characters make and perform in response to events, whether natural or manmade. They do not arise from the events themselves or exist in a character vacuum. In this way, characters serve as the driving forces of the stories that contain them, guiding those stories and propelling them along their paths.

So here is the first small point to be made regarding the *grok approach*, and it's not exactly a stunner. Stories require characters—one in particular.

## CHARACTER SPECTRUM AND CORE ENSEMBLE

The question that naturally follows is: In any story, are all of the characters equal? Does each one supply the same amount of power to the wheels that steer the story and move it forward?

The answer is obviously "no." That's why God created movie extras.

Every story, regardless of its genre, type, or medium, contains a spectrum of characters, from those that fill space and serve as moving props to those that are instrumental to its telling. And just as the electromagnetic spectrum encompasses everything from high-frequency gamma rays to sub-infrared radiation, each region of the character spectrum serves a different purpose—and one region is more useful than the others. In the case of electromagnetic radiation, the spectrum from 400 to 700 nanometers is most useful to human beings, because that is the range of frequencies that our eyes and brains evolved to see. In the case of stories, the most useful part of the spectrum is made up of those characters without whom the story either would not exist or would take a different course—characters who, by virtue of their roles with respect to each other and the plot, steer the story in a given direction or nudge it so that it falls off of one set of tracks and onto another.

It can be reasonably asserted, then, that stories tend to involve a *core ensemble* of characters who are more important than all others. A husband and wife in the midst of a bitter divorce might constitute such characters— as might the young woman who has prompted the husband's infidelity or the wife's best friend and confidant or the tempting pool boy who catches the wife's eye as she considers how to get back at her husband and regain her sense of feeling wanted... or, naturally, the lawyers. (One must never forget the lawyers.)

At first glance, the composition of the *core ensemble* seems almost infinitely variable—a collection of individual parts that can be selected like spices from a rack to season the story without changing its basic recipe. But the *core ensemble* does more than just flavor the story; it supports the story structure and helps to express its *thematic declaration*. And each of its members fills a role that, if left unfilled, would cause the story to head off in a different direction or possibly be rendered incomplete.

So each member of the *core ensemble* is vital to the story, not because of her defining personal characteristics or quirks but because of the role she serves in its telling, such as Ally, Opponent, or Object of Temptation. And just as white light is composed of a wide range of frequencies in the visible part of the spectrum, so each story is informed by every member of its *core ensemble*—one more so than the others.

## THE MOST EQUAL ENSEMBLE MEMBER

Given that the *core ensemble* is the most important part of the character spectrum, the next question is: Are all of its members equal? And again the answer is "no." One member, to paraphrase George Orwell, is more equal than the others by a long shot. So vastly non-equal is this character, in fact, that we bestow on her a title of distinction—"*main character.*"

At Chicago Dramatists, a play development center where I am a resident playwright, every Saturday afternoon is dedicated to the staged reading of a play in progress. The reading is performed script-in-hand, is cast with fine actors (of which the Chicago pool is wide and deep), and might or might not include entrances and exits, at the discretion of the playwright and director.

At the conclusion of every reading, the audience is invited to fill out response sheets that are used to foster discussion in a moderated, after-reading feedback session. The moderator always starts by asking what the audience likes or finds meaningful about the play and moves on from there to possible areas of concern.

One question that sometimes gets asked in the feedback sessions is: Whose play is it? And sometimes neither the audience nor the playwright has a ready answer. Often, an audience member will offer that the play is about the entire ensemble of characters rather than one in particular. And the offering is sometimes met with a communal nodding of heads, as if it represents a holistic, love-your-neighbor, zero-sum approach to storytelling in which no one character has the right to own the story, because the story belongs to the collective. Actors are especially prone to embrace this idea, because they are accustomed to thinking of the roles they play, no matter how small, as vitally important to the piece.

The problem with this line of thinking is that if the story belongs to the collective, then its power to affect any individual audience member through empathetic, one-on-one identification is greatly diminished. The matter of receiving a work of dramatic fiction, like a play or film, is often a communal experience (less so now in the era of streaming video), but each member of the audience receives the story personally, not through the eyes, ears, minds, and opinions of those around him. And the power of any story is determined solely by its member-specific reception. I might share with my friends a common opinion regarding a story, but in the end, I am moved (or not) by how the story touches me personally—not by how it affects the audience as a whole.

In fact, if a story has no *main character*, it is often less a "story" than it is a "tale," by which I mean a sequence of events that might or might not involve a plot. This does not mean that the work has no artistic merit, only that it does not contain the elements that are essential to the creation of a complete story arc. And its weakness involves more than just the natural dilution that arises from the sharing of limited space by multiple characters. It derives from structural matters concerning the work itself.

A fictional work without a *main character* is like a Swiss Army knife. It addresses a multitude of purposes at the expense of the power and refinement that derives from specialization. Personally, if I need to open a can, I'll use a can opener.

Furthermore, the use of an ensemble in lieu of a *main character* does *not* enhance the universality of the story. If a *main character* is organic in her desires and actions, her situation and journey will touch audience members of all types, using nothing more than the language of human universals— fear, joy, despair, pride, and the myriad of other feelings that are common to every member of our species regardless of his culture, age, gender, race, or position in society.

For anecdotal evidence to support this premise, one need look no further than to stories that have struck resonant chords with audiences around the world and across time. From *The Odyssey* (Odysseus) to *Harry Potter and the Sorcerer's Stone* (Harry Potter) to *Chinatown* (Jake Gittes) to *Whale Rider* (Paikea) to *A Christmas Carol* (Ebenezer Scrooge) to *The Lord of the Rings* (Frodo Baggins) to *The Fugitive* (Richard Kimble) to *Romeo and Juliet* (Romeo) to *Casablanca* (Rick Blaine)... to pretty much any powerful and affecting story one can name.

In storytelling, universality requires specificity, not only in the particulars that describe the story world but in the person of the *main character*.

# JOBS OF THE MAIN CHARACTER

It is reasonable to ask at this point: Why is the *main character* so vital to the story? Is it because she gets the most stage-, screen-, speaker-, or page-time and, therefore, must be interesting enough to hold the attention of the audience? Is it because she acts as the psychic glue that binds all of the other characters together and gives them purpose? Is it because most or all of the action in the story revolves around her?

Not really, no.

The *main character* is essential to a well-told story simply because she does most of the heavy lifting in its telling—and not merely by serving as the primary agent and generator of its events. In particular, the *main character* serves four fundamental purposes with respect to the story. She:

- serves as a vehicle through which the audience member can ride along and experience the world of the story;
- generates the story events by means of her *intents* and actions;
- provides the audience with an indicator of story progress; and
- expresses the *theme* of the story by means of her decisions, actions, and ultimate *success* or *failure*.

By any reasonable measure, that's one helluva lot to ask of one character, and yet it is demanded all the time of *main characters* in their stories, regardless of genre, type, or medium. The good ones take on the task and make it look easy.

## MAIN CHARACTER AS STORY VEHICLE

Samuel Taylor Coleridge is credited with first referring to the "willing suspension of disbelief" by the audience in his work *Bibliographia Literaria* (1817). In describing his collaboration with William Wordsworth on the book *Lyrical Ballads, with a Few Other Poems* (1798), he writes:

> "...it was agreed, that my endeavours should be directed to persons and characters supernatural, or at least romantic, yet so as to transfer from our inward nature a human interest and a semblance of truth sufficient to procure for these shadows of imagination that willing suspension of disbelief for the moment, which constitutes poetic faith."

In this passage, he describes the "willing suspension of disbelief" as "poetic faith" (a lovely term) and appeals to it as a means of justifying the use of supernatural elements in his poetry—a practice that had gone out of fashion at the time, swept away by the purported superiority of rationalism. Nowadays, the term "suspended disbelief" is used more broadly to describe the state of complete immersion that the audience member finds himself in when reading, watching, or hearing a story that wraps him up in its world and touches him deeply. One even speaks of "losing" oneself in a story and becoming so completely engrossed in its world that time itself seems to dissolve and disappear. Each page seems to turn on its own, the buttered popcorn vanishes from its tub as if by magic, an uneaten dinner grows cold on the table—all because the audience member is lost in the world of the story and will not be found again until the story ends or takes a break.

To invoke this sort of lost-ness in its audience, a story needs more than mere setting, scenery, and action. It needs a comfortable and well-equipped vehicle into which the audience member can climb, ride along, and experience the journey first-hand. A good story gives its audience member more than a mere telescope to peer into its world and watch the action from afar; it provides him with eyes, ears, and all of the other senses required to fully enter into the story and experience it from within—not *as* a character in the world of the story but *through* such a character. And to convey its world fully, the story must provide access to more than its mere physical dimensions; it must grant admittance to its internal dimensions, as well—the psychological, emotional, and spiritual sensations that give depth to human experience. It must offer a channel of identification and empathy through which the audience member can experience what it is like to live in its world.

In short, it must contain a *main character*.

## MAIN CHARACTER AS STORY GENERATOR

It is a time-worn truism in storytelling circles that to create a compelling story, the writer must ensure that his character *wants* something. As I will show in pages to come, this tired old saw is in need of the severe resharpening that lies at the heart of the *grok approach*, for the simple reason that it is not strictly true—or at least not true enough to provide useful insights into story creation. Even so, it does capsulize the vital aspect of storytelling that I mentioned at the outset of this chapter—that events themselves do not a story make. Stories do more than merely involve their characters, they rely on them and spring from the decisions and actions that arise from their characters' desires.

Here again, the *main character* bears most of the burden. All of the other characters who are more than decoration must desire something, too, of course, even if they are just manning a kiosk in the background. And it is often the conflicts between the characters' desires that generate the conflicts and obstacles in the story.[*] But it is the *main character* whose desire generates the story and moves it forward.

---

[*] Often, but not always. For example, a character may be opposed by Nature herself, who is more than a prop but not a character per se and has no desire. She simply *is*.

In *Chinatown*, it is Jake Gittes's desire to discover and reveal the perpetrator of Hollis Mulray's murder that sets the story course and pulls us onward to its conclusion. Without this desire and Jake's dogged commitment to pursue its fulfillment, the story does not exist. In *A Christmas Carol*, it is Ebenezer Scrooge's desire to remain a stingy, self-absorbed miser that generates the possibilities of the story. If he readily embraced the change of heart recommended to him by Jacob Marley's ghost upon its first appearance in his bedroom, he might be a better person, but the story would never get off the ground. In *Romeo and Juliet*, it is Romeo's youthfully spirited desire for Juliet that gives rise to the conflicts, development, and ultimate *outcome* of the story. If he reckoned that although she was very pretty, he could be just as happy with another girl, especially someone outside the Capulet family, there would be no story.

The *main character* not only steers the story, she creates it.

## MAIN CHARACTER AS INDICATOR OF PROGRESS

An actor friend of mine once asserted to me about theatre, "A play is made up of words *and* movement." She said this after a rehearsal one night to express her dissatisfaction with the way the director had blocked the play she had been rehearsing. She felt that the blocking was too static and had not enough physical movement on the stage.

I remember feeling at the time that her assertion seemed incomplete—a statement that sounds right and reasonable on the surface but reveals itself as hollow the more one explores it. It is true, I thought, that plays involve movement. Static drama is boring drama, and sitting in the audience while a play goes nowhere is worse than watching paint dry. It is like watching paint that has already dried become neither wetter nor dryer.

But anecdotal evidence told me the premise could not be correct. I had seen wonderful works with very little in the way of physical movement. Likewise, I had seen films with action galore that amounted to little more than elaborate fireworks displays. Perhaps the clearest example of this contrast came to me by way of my son when he was six years old and I took him to see the movie *Babe* at a local theatre. He was rapt throughout, his attention riveted to the screen to follow the simple story of a young pig who grows up to win a herding championship meant for dogs only and, in the process, earns the respect and admiration of his owner and fellow barnyard animals. A week or so later, I took him and a five-year-old friend to see the explosion-fest *Batman Forever*. Halfway through the film, both of them were bored to death and far more interested in what was going on around them in the theatre than in what was taking place on the screen.

In pondering my actor-friend's assertion, it occurred to me that plays *are* about movement, but that physical movement is only one of several types of movement possible in a story—others being movement internal to the characters (spiritual, emotional, or psychological), changes in the external state of the story world, and movement of the plot itself.

The reason that my son and his friend were bored in *Batman Forever* is that a large percentage of screen time was taken up with flashy falderal that served no great purpose in advancing the story. The story was spinning its wheels in grand fashion, throwing sparks in every direction as it dug itself into the storytelling mud. And my son and his friend knew it, as children do forthrightly. *Babe*, on the other hand, offered a constant sense of progress as each new scene pulled the audience further along, gave it insight into the characters, and moved the story forward.

So how do you impart a sense of movement to a story? Simple. You give it a *main character* who holds in her mind (consciously or not) a definable *goal*. The race that will be won or lost by its end. The murderer who will either be discovered and brought to trial or will slip off into oblivion. The love interest whose affections will either be confirmed by an "I do" at the altar or lost to the arms of a rival.

Why is it important to give the *main character* a definable *goal*? Because by doing so, you give the audience a means of measuring the story progress. Specifically, you define a marker of ultimate achievement. Whenever we-the-audience sense that the *main character* is progressing toward the *goal*, we feel as if we are moving forward. Whenever we sense movement away from the *goal*, either by virtue of a temporary setback or complete reversal, we feel as if we are moving backward. And whenever the *goal* appears to be getting neither nearer nor farther away, we feel a sense of stasis which, if allowed to fester, leads to boredom.

It is important to keep in mind here that the sense of movement created by any story occurs and is generated solely within the mind of the audience member and relies on his expectations for its traction. When you install in your story a *main character* who possesses a measurable *goal*, you give the audience a way of determining progress. And by doing so, you impart the sense of movement to the story.

The measurable *goal* is so critical to story creation, in fact, that it helps to define an important milestone in the story—the end of the first structural act[*]. Simply put, when we-the-audience know who the *main character* is, what she *intends* to accomplish in the story (and *why*), and how we are to measure her *success* or *failure*, Act I is over and Act II has begun.

And yes, it really is as simple as that.

---

[*] I am drawing a distinction here between the internal structure of a story and its outward appearance. For example, a well-constructed two-act play actually contains three structural acts—Act I, Act II, and Act III. Typically, the audience members get up to visit the restrooms, check their cell phones, and purchase concessions somewhere in the middle of Act II.

## MAIN CHARACTER AS BEARER OF THE THEME

Another question that is often asked in the after-reading discussions at Chicago Dramatists is: What is the play about? Which is another way of posing the question: What is its *theme*?

This question is often met with the furrowing of brows as audience members ponder how to express concisely the overall message they derived from watching the play. The answers, when finally offered, are typically thoughtful. If they suffer from anything, it is a soft, amorphous vagueness and lack of specificity. And since the audiences for the Saturday readings are generally well-read and, in many cases, accustomed to working with words, the vagueness is clearly not the result of lack of intelligence or facility of expression. It stems, rather, from the fact that no one has ever created a grammar specifically designed to express a story *theme*.

Until now.

As I will show in Part Two of this book, the questions regarding story *theme* can be answered confidently, emphatically, enthusiastically, and concretely by means of a grammar I developed as an outgrowth of the *grok approach* and refer to as *thematic imprinting*. And deep at the core of *thematic imprinting* stands our friend the *main character*. It is her story we watch unfold as we turn the pages, gaze at the television screen, or lean forward in our seats at the theatre. And just as we gauge the story progress according to the signposts that lead to her ultimate *goal*, we parse the *theme* of the story by judging the merit of that *goal* in conjunction with its ultimate *outcome*.

But all that is to follow. For the moment, I'll leave it at this:

The *main character*—vehicle of transport through the story world, generator of the story itself, and indicator of its progress—is also the bearer of its *theme*.

As I mentioned at the outset of this chapter, the *main character* does all of the heavy lifting in the story, which is why she must be well-crafted to make the story work. The nice thing about this fact of storytelling life is that if you encounter difficulty with any aspect of your story during its creation or development, you now know the first place to look.

# Chapter 3

## ACTION, MOVEMENT, AND INTENT

As I noted in Chapter 2, stories involve many kinds of movement—physical, spiritual, emotional, psychological, and that which is related to progression of the plot. In a well-told story, such movements do not simply appear in the sky like angels and gently alight to move the story forward. They are created by characters engaging in actions. The actions might be *external*, such as taking cover from flying bullets or lying on a couch and petting heavily. Or they might be *internal*, such as deciding to invite a potential paramour to a dinner party or steeling oneself against the insults of a friend-turned-enemy. But regardless of their nature, they spring to life at the turbulent confluence of desire and opportunity and manifest as an outgrowth of *intent*. Therefore, deep at the core of the movement in any story lies *intent*—specifically that of the *main character*.

## ACTION VERSUS MOVEMENT

Just as a sequence of events does not make a story, so action by itself is not movement. A boy juggling baseballs might capture our attention, but his actions do not constitute story movement unless they are paired with motivation. Throw a love interest into the mix and put her in the audience watching the performance, and the potential for story movement starts to swirl around him. Seat the love interest next to another boy whom we know to be her current boyfriend, and now we have the makings of a scene. The juggling boy is not only trying to impress his love interest, he is trying to win her away from a rival.

The introduction of the love interest gives us a complete movement to watch. Not just baseballs flying through the air but an *attempt* by a boy to impress a girl he is sweet on. And by placing her in proximity to a rival, we heighten the importance of his *success* and thrust a question into the scene: Will he or won't he perform well enough to win her away from the other boy? Or to state things more universally: Will he or won't he *succeed*?

It is this unanswered question that keeps us focused on the scene while it plays out and imbues it with a sense of movement. The boy might juggle masterfully, but is he good enough to accomplish his *goal* regarding the girl? That is the question at hand.

12

And the question itself raises an important point about storytelling—that when it comes to conveying information of any kind, questions trump explanations every time. It is far more effective to create a question that we-the-audience need to have answered than it is to try to push information into our collective mind. Why? Because our species is curious by nature. Somewhere in our genetic coding is a thing that gets hooked by the unanswered question. And it is that thing that keeps our eyes glued to the page, screen, or stage when we find ourselves caught up in a story. If the writer poses a question that intrigues us, we are driven to pay attention until the answer is revealed. Not only that, the more significant the question, the harder we pay attention. That's just how we are. Blame Nature.

By creating a dramatic question—for example, "Will the boy perform well enough to win the affections of the girl?"—the writer creates an informational void that we-the-audience will want to see filled. And that is what will keep us following the flights of the baseballs through the air—not the beauty of the juggling act itself but the question regarding whether any of them will drop and, if so, what will that mean for the boy and his hopes of winning the affections of the girl.

So when it comes to creating a scene and its details, the writer has two basic methods at his disposal. He can present information for the taking—describing things that happen and hoping that they are interesting enough to catch and hold the attention of the audience. Or he can pose a dramatic question, thereby creating an informational void and playing to the I-must-know addiction of our species.

As a general rule, it's hard to go wrong playing to someone's addiction.

## WANT VERSUS INTENT

First, allow me to dismiss the many deceptive synonyms of *wanting*. They simply don't belong in this discussion. When I speak about *wanting* in the context of storytelling, I do not mean any of the airy imposters that dress up like *wanting* but do not motivate action. *Wishing*, for example, is not *wanting*. Neither is *hoping* or *pining*. In the context of the *grok approach*, *wanting* means possessing a desire strong enough to prompt pursuit of its satisfaction—or, to use an important rewording, possessing a desire that is capable of spawning an *intent*.

And with that important distinction in hand, we can at last go to work on the old saw I mentioned in Chapter 2—the one that says a well-crafted story must include a character who *wants* something. Specifically, it is time to abandon the notion that what matters in a story is what the *main character wants* and to replace it with a truer, more-potent notion—a notion with sharper teeth. And here it is:

In storytelling, it does not matter what the *main character wants*;
what matters is what she *intends*.

And the difference between the two terms is more than semantic. It is
the difference between vagueness and specificity, inaction and action, stasis
and movement. One can sit in a lotus position on a mountaintop in Tibet
cut off from all of humanity and *want* something. But if one *intends* something, one must put on one's work gloves and get dirty. One must *attempt*
to bring about the *goal* of the *intent*. And it is the playing out of the *attempt*
that creates the story and its movement.

A *want* says, "I would really like to see something happen to satisfy
this desire of mine. Yessir, that would be great." An *intent* says, "I will take
steps to satisfy this desire of mine, and I won't give up until it is clear that I
have either *succeeded* or that *success* is impossible."

A respected surgeon wrongly convicted of murdering his wife might
*want* to live in a world where his innocence is public knowledge and the
identity of the killer is known, but unless he seizes the chance to make that
world a reality when the opportunity arises and *intends* to find out and
reveal who killed his wife and why, he simply bides his time in prison,
without either his freedom or a tell-able story. A young man with a mixed-
results amateur boxing record might *want* to attain the sense of respect that
has never been his, but unless he *intends* to do so when the opportunity presents itself and hones his body and skills to carry out his *intent*, the first-
round bell of the fight of his life never rings. A nightclub owner whose past
contains painful romantic memories that have caused him to cocoon himself in a psychological shell might *want* to maintain his jaded neutrality in
the face of the unexpected reappearance of his lost love—but unless he
*intends* to keep his embittered world intact, and takes the steps necessary to
do so, there is no story.

*Wants* may spawn *intents*, but it is the *intents* themselves that prompt
actions on the part of the characters who possess them and thereby generate
movement in the story. Without *intent*, there is no story. Period.

In this way, *intents* can be thought of as filters, separating red-blooded
*wants* from their anemic, lackadaisical cousins. The deceptive synonyms of
*wanting* do not spawn *intents*.

## THE LENS OF INTENT

The recognition of *intent* as the true source of motivated movement
provides the writer with a powerful lens for peering into his story all the
way to its bones and bloodstream and examining its soul. How so? Because
*intents* are associated with specific *goals*, and the *goal* of the *main character*
in any story serves three primary functions. Specifically, it:

- generates purposeful action on the part of the *main character*;
- provides the audience with a means to measure story progress; and
- produces a *course of action* that can be judged by the audience, thereby establishing and expressing the story *theme*.

So the mere act of thinking in terms of *intents* instead of *wants* lays the groundwork from which we can begin to construct a new approach to creating and developing stories—because it forces us to rephrase (read: phrase correctly) the fundamental question regarding the *main character* and her role in the story. To reiterate that bit of correct phrasing, the fundamental question when examining or developing a story is not: What does the character *want?* The fundamental question is: What does the character *intend?*

And now that the question is properly posed, our visas are stamped and the border guards are waving us into the realm of the *grok approach*.

# Chapter 4

## FOUNDATIONS OF THE *grok* APPROACH

### LESSONS FROM NATURE

To illustrate the organic nature of the *grok approach*, we begin its derivation in the realm of the humble *Euglena*, a unicellular aquatic organism whose behavior exhibits mixed characteristics of both animals and plants. Its animal-like characteristics include a thin, whip-like strand that allows it to move from place to place. Its plant-like characteristics include a light-sensitive "eyespot" on one end and the ability to produce its own food by photosynthesis.

If you place a hungry *Euglena* into a water-filled Petri dish and expose only part of the dish to light, the *Euglena* will sense the light and try to move toward it, so that it can satisfy its hunger. If you move it away from the light before it is fully sated, it will do its best to return to the light, and it will resist your efforts to move it away in the first place.

Now, let us move a bit higher on the evolutionary ladder.

Many animals, such as the red-breasted lemur, the Western fence lizard, and well... *homo sapiens*, exhibit territorial behavior. A territorial animal invests time and energy to create a treasured place in its environment, such as a nest or feeding ground, and will defend that place, as necessary, even from other members of its own species. Such acts of defense tend to center on colorful displays, boisterous calls, and shows of aggression rather than on physical conflict (except in the case of *homo sapiens*). But despite the differences in strategies and tactics, the acts share a common objective—to maintain possession of a treasured place that the animal has created for itself. And if the animal is driven away from its treasured place by a usurper, it may well return at a later date and try to retake possession, depending on its level of desperation and the availability of alternatives.

So far, so good. Let us climb another rung or two on that ladder.

At the start of any American football game, the score is tied at 0–0. From that point forward, the two competing teams share a common overarching *goal*—to be in possession of the scoreboard lead when the game clock expires. So if one looks at the game strictly from the standpoint of possession, the *goal* of each team at any point in the contest can be expressed in terms of a single treasured item—the scoreboard lead.

When the game begins, each team has the same short-term objective—to obtain the treasured item that it has not heretofore possessed (the scoreboard lead). But as soon as one team scores, its objective changes, because it now possesses the treasured item and must strive to preserve its possession. It might do so by trying to score again or by trying to keep the other team from scoring at all, depending on relative strengths of the two teams. But regardless of its strategies and tactics, the short-term objective of the team that scores first is always the same, namely to preserve its possession of the treasured item that it has successfully obtained.

The opposing team, on the other hand, will maintain its initial objective even after the first points are scored—that is, to obtain the lead that it has (still) not yet possessed. And it will continue to maintain that objective until it succeeds in doing so, at which point the treasured item (the lead) will be in its possession, and it will be compelled to change its own strategies and tactics to preserve its newfound ownership.

Finally, when the team that scored first falls behind for the first time, it will direct its efforts to reacquiring possession of the treasured item it once possessed—that precious lead.

That is the nature of a football game in a nutshell. Two teams battling to obtain a treasured item that neither possesses at the start of the contest and to be found in possession of that item when the whistle blows to signal the end of the game. First, both teams *attempt* to *gain* possession of the treasured item that neither has yet possessed. Then, when one team succeeds in doing so, it must *attempt* to *keep* possession of the treasured item in the face of its opponent's efforts to take it away. And if the team that scored first loses possession of the treasured item at some point, it must *attempt* to *regain* it before time runs out in the game.

Not a fan of American football? Okay. Substitute soccer, baseball, polo, curling, or war—a large part of which typically involves obtaining control of real estate, retaking real estate the control of which has been lost, and defending real estate currently controlled.

Welcome to the *grok approach*, a new way of thinking about characters and stories. An approach derived from Nature itself and the struggles of its creatures to survive. An elementary approach to sussing motivations and using them to probe the depths of any story and its characters. An approach that echoes Frank Lloyd Wright's fundamental aesthetic of "organic architecture" because it leads to the creation of stories that "fit naturally in their places."

An approach the foundations of which are rooted firmly in the logical bedrock of Nature by means of three fundamental *types of intent*.

## TYPES OF INTENT

If we consider the cases cited above, we observe that at every step on the evolutionary ladder, the objective of a living entity (if we treat the football team as a single entity) with respect to a *treasure* (an item or state of affairs that it considers valuable) can be described in one of three ways—to:

· obtain a *treasure* that it has never possessed,

· reacquire a *treasure* that it previously possessed, or

· hold onto a *treasure* that it currently possesses.

The *Euglena* moves toward the lighted region of its Petri dish (its *treasure*) so that it can nourish itself. If displaced from that region, it *attempts* to return. And it *attempts* to resist displacement in the first place.

The territorial animal expends energy to create a *treasure* that does not exist (and, therefore, it has never possessed)—for example, a nest or breeding ground. If its possession of that *treasure* is threatened, it acts to defend and preserve it. And if it loses possession and lives to see another day, it may refuse to accept defeat and *attempt* to retake possession of the *treasure* it created and once owned.

At the start of the game, the football team *attempts* to obtain the *treasure* it has not yet possessed—the scoreboard lead. If it succeeds in doing so, it *attempts* to maintain that possession against the efforts of its opponent, which seeks the *treasure* for its own. And if it loses the short-term struggle, it must *attempt* to reacquire the *treasure* before the clock runs out and its opportunity to do so disappears.

These are simple examples from three very different rungs of the evolutionary ladder, all exhibiting a common set of objectives. A trio of purposes (*types of intent*) that can be summarized in the following manner—to:

· *gain* a *treasure* that one has never possessed,

· *regain* a *treasure* that one possessed previously, or

· *keep* a *treasure* that one currently possesses.

To *gain*, *regain*, or *keep*.

To *grok*.

And now you know the essence of the *grok approach*.

# THE NUTSHELL AND ITS CHEWY CENTER

Simply put, the *grok approach** is based on the idea that the *main character* in any story is motivated by a single overarching objective and that the objective can be expressed in terms of one of three possible *types of intent*. Specifically, the *main character* can *intend* to either:

- *gain* a *treasure* that she has never possessed,
- *regain* a *treasure* that she previously possessed, or
- *keep* a *treasure* that she currently possesses.

And any audience member who invests his attention in the story does so to discover one thing—whether the *main character* will *succeed* or *fail* in her *attempt* to *gain*, *regain*, or *keep* the *treasure*. Side stories and characters may abound and enrich the story, casting colorful lights and defining shadows throughout, but we-the-audience stay seated inside the vehicle of the *main character* as she traverses the story world simply because we hope to discover the ultimate *succeed*-or-*fail outcome* at the end of the ride.

That is the chewy center that lies at the heart of the *grok approach*, at least in terms of its minute-to-learn-and-lifetime-to-apply underpinnings. Like a fundamental equation of physics, it is simple, elegant, and useful—a straightforward jumping-off point for understanding any story at its most basic level. And that understanding, in turn, allows the writer to create stories that are rich and structurally sound and to demolish the unnecessary decoration that can threaten to choke the beauty of a story as it develops, so that the final product may fairly gleam.

In short, the *grok approach* is the sacred crystal from which soulful story knowledge streams if only the writer knows the secret code that unlocks the knowledge.

Here's a hint: The code involves three letters.

---

* The *grok approach* takes its name from the acronym formed by the phrase *"gain, regain, or keep,"* but it also pays homage to the word first coined by Robert Heinlein in his 1961 science fiction novel, *Stranger in a Strange Land*, where it was said to have been of Martian origin, meaning (in one sense), "To understand profoundly through intuition or empathy," which fairly sums up what the *grok approach* is about.

# Chapter 5

## EXPLORING THE *grok* APPROACH

Now, we come to the "so what." Or to state the matter in loftier terms, we begin to explore the panoply of ramifications that result from application of the *grok approach*. (So much for loftier terms.) The *grok approach* is, in fact, rife with ramifications, some of which are story-specific and many of which apply to everyday life. And although they touch every aspect of storytelling, they affect two aspects most strongly:

- Development of the *main character*
- Construction of the story

With regard to the development of the *main character*, the *grok approach* helps to identify her true motivation and ensure that it is plausible in the context of the story world. It also helps to promote consistency in her actions, so that everything she does makes sense in light of who she is and what drives her. With regard to story construction, the *grok approach* provides important insights into matters such as its "time frame of concern," its structural points of reference, and the manner in which its progress is defined. The approach also reveals commonalities between seemingly disparate stories and draws parallels between the strategies and tactics employed by their characters.

Because the construction of any story depends heavily on the *main character* for its particulars, it is not possible to explore these two aspects in isolation from each other. By addressing them as distinct subjects, however, it is possible to highlight important facets of each and to cross-reference those facets where necessary.

## DEVELOPMENT OF THE MAIN CHARACTER

As I mentioned in Chapter 2, the *main character* does most of the work in the telling of any story. Consequently, the savvy writer must focus on her development as a primary means of crafting the story itself. The *grok approach* helps him to do so by directly addressing three important tasks:

- Identifying her true motivation
- Ensuring the plausibility of her *intent*
- Promoting consistency in her actions

The first of these tasks uses the *grok approach* to pinpoint the primary drive behind the actions of the *main character*, especially with respect to its effects on the story. The second keeps the story grounded in its own reality and uses the rules of that reality to reveal the deepest *intent* of the *main character*. The third ensures that the *main character* is coherent in her actions and behaviors from beginning to end.

## IDENTIFYING TRUE MOTIVATION

The first and most obvious consequence of the *grok approach* is that it allows us to recast the fundamental question regarding the motivation of the *main character* in terms that are truly useful. Specifically, it permits us to restate the objective that spawns the story *goal*. Armed with the *grok approach*, we can take down the tired old saw about what the *main character wants* and hammer it into a gleaming machete that we can use to cut away the underbrush of a story and find our way to its center. And when we do so, we get a very concrete and revealing question about the story. A question that requires a very specific answer—the kind of answer that leads to revelations and the solving of story problems.

To restate the main point of Chapter 3, it is the *intent* of the *main character* that serves as the fundamental driving force in any story. Recognition of this fact allows us to recast the question regarding what a character *wants* into its more-powerful counterpart: What does the *main character intend?* The *grok approach* allows us to further expand and enhance this question, so that it becomes: What *treasure* does the *main character intend* to *gain*, *regain*, or *keep*?

And it is from this properly posed question that a fruitful exploration of the *main character* and her motivations can be launched.

For one thing, this form of the question narrows the field of possibilities regarding what can drive the actions and behaviors of the *main character*— so that the writer is not left drifting without a paddle as he tries to navigate a mind-boggling reef of alternatives in search of the fundamental, story-driving motivation. The question can and must be answered as simply as it is stated—for example, "The *main character* in this story *intends* to *gain* X," where X is the *treasure* that she has never possessed (possibly because it has yet to exist) or "The *main character* in this story intends to *keep* Y," where Y is the *treasure* that she currently possesses but is under threat of losing (perhaps because it might be destroyed). At the same time, however, the properly posed question expands the field of possibilities from which the answers can be drawn, because the term "*treasure*" can apply to not only physical items but non-physical items, as well—for example, a position of honor, a sense of self-worth, or family unity.

For another thing, the question demands specificity in its answer—which is always a good thing in storytelling, because it provides the audience with tangible touch points that focus its attention and shut out the non-story world. In short, the more specific elements there are in a story, the less likely it is that the audience will look for excuses to abandon its poetic faith. The demand for specificity also compels the writer to dig deep into the soul of the *main character* to discover the *treasure* that will truly satisfy her *intent*—thereby helping his audience to identify with her quest. It is one thing to hear of a "woman who has family troubles" and quite another to hear of a "mother who is grappling with her 10-year-old daughter's addiction to cocaine." In any story, it is the details that flesh out the matter at hand and render it real enough to capture our attention.

## Avoiding Superficial Motivations

When introducing the *grok approach* to my classes, I often begin by invoking the old saw that a compelling character must *want* something and asking the question: So what can a character *want*? And more often than not (and I mean *really* more often than not), the number-one answer is money, followed closely by power and love.

Characters trying to acquire money (*yawn*), power (*yawn*), or (less so, but still... *yawn*) love. These objectives represent the first three whistle stops on the Old-Saw Express to Cliché-town.

And that, in a nutshell, illustrates the fundamental problem with the old saw itself—the fact that its question can be answered either vaguely or with a worn-out conceptual object that might or might not motivate a *course of action*. Consequently, the question gets us nowhere, and its posing can actually hinder story development.

Has a compelling story ever been told that involved the pursuit of money? Certainly. How is that possible? Because the money itself served as nothing more than a means of fulfilling some deeper need—for example, as a *trophy* to establish a positive self-image, a resource to heal a loved one, or a method of safeguarding others. In each case, however, the money is simply the means to an end, and it is the end itself that contains the fundamental motivation for the *main character*.

In the first case (that of the *trophy*), for example, the money serves as a placating icon—something the *main character* pursues to *gain* the feeling that she is "okay." Which means that her actual *treasure* is "feeling okay." And if that feeling could be obtained by means having nothing to do with money, the money itself would be moot. This is the hidden truth that lies at the heart of any story wherein a *main character* pursues wealth and discovers along the way that other aspects of life are at least as important if not more so.

In the second case (a resource to heal a loved one), the actual *treasure* for the *main character* involves the health of a loved one, and the money represents nothing more than a means of bringing about the healing. If the loved one could be healed by some means not involving money—for example, by the magical touch of a shaman—or the *main character* could free herself from desiring the healing in the first place (which might be advisable if the loved one is faking the illness to prey upon her compassionate nature), the importance of the money and its pursuit would simply vanish.

And in the third case (a method of safeguarding others), the money again is nothing more than one type of means to an end. There are many ways to safeguard others, depending on the nature of the threat. And even if money is the only viable means of providing the safety, it remains nothing more than a tool that must be acquired for that purpose. The actual *treasure* for the *main character* derives from the significance of the others she feels compelled to safeguard and the threat to their well-being. The story is about *keeping* them protected, not *gaining* the money to do it.

Replace the word "money" with "power" in this discussion, and the significant points of the argument do not change. The two most common answers to the old-saw question (money and power) may constitute excellent signposts for the gauging of progress in a story, but as sources of true motivation they actually suck.

Love is a slightly different animal in this regard, because the word itself contains the implication of personal need and suggests a form of deep, internal motivation. Even here, however, the vagueness of the answer to the old-saw question cripples its effectiveness in identifying the true motivation of the *main character*. Love has many modes and forms—for example, it may be given, received, parental, platonic, or erotic. By demanding specificity in its answer, the properly posed question requires the writer to consider the many forms and modes of love and helps him to identify those most suited to the *intent* of his *main character*.

## Distinguishing Between Getting and Gaining

But there is another, deeper, problem with the old saw that can now be examined in the bright and unforgiving light of the *grok approach*—that is, its tendency to focus on "getting" as a fundamental driving force in stories and to elevate characters who exhibit the "desire to get" (read: compulsion to acquire) to the rank of "Strong and Interesting People Worth Caring About." Such characters are granted positions of glory in the conventional storytelling world largely because the word "want" is so closely associated with the word "get" in modern use. So, for many writers, the question "What does my character *want*?" is identical to asking "What does my character *want* to get?"

The problem, of course, is that not all characters *want* to get something—and those who do often represent the antithesis of strength, regardless of how passionate they are about their desires. Consequently, we-the-audience may find them mildly entertaining to observe from afar, but they are crippled in their ability to lure us inside themselves for the journey into the Land of Poetic Faith.[*]

The *grok approach*, on the other hand, reveals that getting is just one form of *gaining* and that *gaining* is only one of three possible *types of intent*—the others being *regaining* and *keeping*. And the recognition of this distinction greatly expands the ways in which a writer can think about his *main character* and increases the numbers and types of motivations at his disposal.

Life is not merely about getting. Sometimes it is about retrieving what one once possessed or holding on to what one has. And even when it is about getting, it is often about doing so on behalf of someone else or all of humanity.

The old-saw question does not explicitly honor those possibilities. The *grok approach* does.

## ENSURING PLAUSIBILITY OF INTENT

When relating a story, every writer asks implicitly for the audience to grant him a bit of poetic faith—that gift of suspended disbelief that is so necessary for the world of the story to seem real and engaging. And we-the-audience are typically quite generous in our granting of such faith, in part because we recognize that it is necessary to our participation in the experience of the story. We also tend to be generous because we know that we are responsible for having created the encounter in the first place—by opening the book, walking into the theatre, or pressing the start button on the video remote control. It is rare that an audience member is dragged into a story against his will. One can think of instances, of course—for example, the young man who takes his girlfriend to a "chick flick" either to advance the courting process or to keep the domestic peace. And the next young woman who reluctantly accompanies her boyfriend to a film replete with explosions, blood, and death will not be the first to have done so.

---

[*] One unfortunate offshoot of old-saw thinking is the idea that the most interesting characters are those who are opportunistic and exhibit *proactive* tendencies. With few exceptions, this premise is false. In point of fact, the most interesting and sympathetic characters are often those who are *reactive*—that is, who respond to the challenges and opportunities that come their way without being directly sought after. The *proactive* psychotic killer on the prowl for a new victim is far less likely to hold our attention than is his next target, who finds herself *reacting* in a do-or-die struggle for life, or the investigator who *reacts* to the crime spree by attempting to find and capture the killer before he murders again.

Once that poetic faith is granted, however, the burden of nurturing and maintaining it rests entirely on the shoulders of the writer, and the audience is absolved of all further responsibility. As a matter of fact, we-the-audience are likely to keep a wary eye on the underpinnings of the story as it plays out, looking for cracks and flaws, largely because the granting of faith is not without cost. It takes time to watch or listen to a show or read a book—which is why a disgruntled audience member will sometimes express his frustration in terms of, "Well, there's two hours of my life I'll never get back." And no one likes to make a bad investment. We-the-audience want our poetic faith to pay off with insight and internal movement or, at the very least, entertainment enough to remove us from the real world for a while.

To ensure a fruitful return on the investment of his audience, the writer must keep cracks in the story to a minimum and eliminate them completely, if possible. One aspect of doing so requires him to ensure that the *intent* of the *main character* is plausible within the story world. In this regard, the *grok approach* is especially helpful, because it forces the writer to think in terms of what *treasure* (item or state of being) the *main character* can reasonably *intend* to *gain*, *regain*, or *keep*. Such thinking, in turn, demands a thorough examination of the *main character* and the asking of questions that give the story focus and direction. And doing so is more than a mere exercise; it is the discipline that helps the writer to ignore the phantom desires that lead to dead ends and to find, instead, the true, plausible *intent* of the *main character*, by which I mean the *intent* that creates a robust and compelling story.

As a simple example, consider a scenario in which the *main character* is a middle-aged housewife who has recently suffered the sudden loss of the husband she adored. The funeral is over and the well-wishers have gone their way, leaving her to grapple with a day-to-day existence unlike she has known in many years—waking up alone each morning and cooking meals for only herself. The loss of the husband has ripped from her the comfortable routines and simple joys that had come to define her daily existence.

On your mark... Get set... Storytell!

At the start of the story creation process, the life of our widow is defined by the loss of the relationship she used to enjoy. It is easy to conceive of such a character and to fill in the blanks when it comes to her state of mind and likely behaviors. She is sad, and we don't blame her. Most of us know how it feels to lose someone you love, and we can certainly ride along in the vehicle of her pain.

Sadness? Been there and brought back refrigerator magnets. Paralyzing loneliness? Took the guided tour. Emotional desolation? Didn't need the map in the back of the book. Drew my own on a restaurant napkin and handed it off to a young couple from Austria as I left the site and climbed back onto the bus.

The point is that unless you are an emotionless sociopath reading this book in your cell between shock treatments, it is not hard to empathize with the plight of the widow. Her world has been torn apart, and it is natural for us to feel sorry for her.

But the mere illustration of her sadness does not make for an interesting story. In fact, from a storytelling standpoint, her sadness is completely irrelevant except insofar as it serves to create an *intent* that will lead to a journey. It is not enough to show us that she is sad. To be worthy of our investment of poetic faith, the writer must show us the *intent* that springs from her sadness and not only sets the story on its rails but lights the coal in its firebox to get it going. In short, it is neither entertaining nor enlightening to watch our widow lament the loss of her husband; she could sit in a hut in the mountains of Tibet and do that. The story lies in what happens in the aftermath of her loss, which, in turn, depends on her *intent*.

So the first question the writer must ask is: What is it about the *main character* and her sadness that could generate a powerful *intent*? And the answer, to be valid and useful, must obey one simple rule:

> The *main character* is not allowed to *intend* anything that is impossible in the world of the story.

The implications of this rule are profound, because it forces the writer to define clearly the parameters of the story world and what is allowable within it—and thereby helps him to focus on what the *main character* can reasonably *intend*. In the case of the widow, for example, regardless of how deeply she misses her husband, she cannot *intend* to *regain* "the life they had together" unless the writer is willing to incorporate non-realistic elements in the story. In the ordinary world of day-to-day life, the husband is not coming back, and if the writer is unwilling to incorporate fantasy or science fiction, the widow cannot hope to return to the life she enjoyed with her husband. Consequently, any longing she may possess to do so will result in an unworkable *intent*. In this way, the rules of the story world help define her *intent* by narrowing the range of its possibilities.

Interesting... very interesting.

But what if the writer is unwilling to incorporate fantasy or science fiction in the world of the widow, which is probably a smart choice, given the likely audience for the story? What if he insists on placing the story in what we commonly regard as the real world—the world we are likely to encounter if we put on our jackets and head down the street for breakfast at the local café. What then?

The answer is that he can still use the widow and the loss of her husband as the basis of the story, but he must keep a wary eye on her *intent* to ensure that it is plausible in that world. And the *grok approach* demands that he think not only in terms of what the widow *intends*, but in specific terms regarding the *treasure* that she can reasonably *intend* to *gain*, *regain*, or *keep*.

So let's do that.

When considering what *treasure* the widow could *intend* to *gain*, for example, one possibility that presents itself is a "coming to terms with the new normal." Anyone who has ever been abruptly dislodged from his day-to-day lifestyle has been challenged to adopt new rules, routines, and ways of thinking and to thereby construct an existence within a "new normal." Some of us do so by imposing our old ways of thinking as best we can; others embrace the new reality and try to change themselves to fit in. Regardless of approach, however, the deftness with which a person meets the challenge can mean the difference between happiness or sadness, joy or depression, and (sometimes) life or death.

The precise definition of what it means to "come to terms with the new normal" is entirely at the discretion of the writer. For one writer, the widow might seek to honor the memory of her husband in some special way and to make lemonade from what she rightly sees as the massive sour fruit she has been handed. For another, the widow might struggle to cope with her loss—to seek professional help or that of friends, to develop hobbies or go back to work, or to keep her hours filled so that she does not have to think about the loss.

And keep in mind that just because the widow possesses an *intent*, nothing demands that she *succeed* in her *attempt* to realize its *goal*. It is quite possible, for example, to construct a story in which her upbringing forbade the expression of emotions, especially those related to pain or weakness. If she hails from such a background, she might attack the challenge of finding a new normal with what amounts to an elaborate program of "doing" by keeping herself occupied to avoid confronting any uncomfortable feelings she might possess. And if she *fails* in her efforts to construct the new normal in this way, she might be forced to recognize the inherent weakness of such avoidance and to confront, perhaps for the first time, feelings that she had long suppressed or denied. Her *failure*, in that case, might open the door to a life of self-realization and deepened human experience—in other words, a better life.*

Now, that might be a story worth watching.

---

* Contrary to the annoyingly popular modern expression of public bravado that, "Failure is not an option," for the writer *failure* is very definitely an option and is often, in fact, the best choice for a story, depending on its *theme* (see Part Two).

But what if the writer wants to grant the widow an *intent* that involves *regaining* instead of *gaining*? The question becomes, then: What *treasure* can she reasonably *intend* to *regain*? As I noted above, in the absence of fantasy or science fiction, she cannot *intend* to *regain* the life that she enjoyed with her late husband. So what is left?

Hmmm…

How about the life she lived before she and her husband were married? Maybe, for example, she had sacrificed a successful career for marriage, and as much as she loved her husband while he was alive, his death provides her with the opportunity to return to (*regain*) that career—with all of its differences, good and bad, from the life to which she had become accustomed. And maybe here again she *fails* and realizes that the marriage has changed her too much to go back to the life she had before. Or maybe changes in the professional world have rendered the skills she used before obsolete, and the profession no longer needs her.

Or maybe to *regain* a sense of romantic worth, she invites the attentions of a paramour, *intent* on recapturing the passion she felt with her husband when they were young. And perhaps the paramour differs from her husband in ways that make the recapturing impossible, thereby forcing her to either give up the quest or come to terms with a new normal in which she may need to pursue a different kind of love.

And please notice an important difference between the new normal that results from this *regain* scenario and that of the *gain* scenario outlined above. In the *gain* scenario, attaining the new normal constitutes the *intent* of the *main character* and, therefore, serves as the gauge by which we-the-audience measure progress in the story and determine *success* or *failure*. In this *regain* scenario, the new normal is a *consequence* of *failure*, not a *goal* of an *intent*; therefore, it is not used during the story to measure progress or judge its *outcome*.

Or what if instead of *gaining* or *regaining*, the writer assigns the widow the task of *keeping* something? What *treasure* could she *intend* to *keep*? The most obvious, perhaps, is a sense of faithfulness to her husband. Perhaps, for example, her identity is so intimately tied to him that to abandon devotion to his memory—maybe in the face of advice from caring friends who see it imprisoning her—would mean the complete destruction of the person she considers herself to be. And again perhaps she *fails* to achieve the *goal* of *keeping* faithful (as she originally defines it) and comes to realize that life must go on even after his death. Or perhaps she *succeeds* and by doing so closes herself off from emotional growth—which might constitute a recipe for even greater sadness.

So here we have several scenarios, each of which involves a *main character* who can be described generically as a middle-aged widow. The resulting stories differ greatly from each other due largely to the differences in their *types of intent*, yet each of them could easily serve as the basis of a rich and wonderful story rather than a mere examination of her pain. Thanks, in part, to the *grok approach*.

The point here is that the *grok approach* demands a specific *intent* on the part of the *main character*, and the *intent* must be plausible in the world of the story. That restriction leaves the writer with a choice between two alternatives—either change the world of the story so that the *intent* of the *main character* is plausible within its rules or examine the *main character* to find an *intent* that fits the rules as they are. Neither alternative is superior to the other, but the choice affects everything about the story, including the challenges faced by the *main character*, the consequences of *success* and *failure*, and the story *theme*.

## PROMOTING CONSISTENCY IN ACTION

It sometimes happens when watching, reading, or hearing a story that the audience observes a character who seems forced or allowed to do something that is either against her nature or has nothing to do with her journey. That something might make sense from a rational standpoint and might even represent the most direct mode of action given her immediate circumstances. Still, it seems somehow false, and not in a way that characterizes her. The action seems truly false—born in the realm of poor storytelling.

Such falsehoods, whether momentary and passing or sticky and permanent, often result from pesky disconnects that occur in the mind of the writer during creation and development of the story. And without a ready means of diagnosis and treatment, they can end up in the final story, where the audience is left to feel them as minor offenses to its sensibilities and lose, if only for a moment, its poetic faith. In this regard, the *grok approach* serves as both the means of diagnosis and the cure—the MRI test and the scalpel, the incubated culture and the serum-filled syringe… the bathroom scale and the exercise machine. Because it allows the writer to do two things:

· Identify a characteristic *type of intent* for the *main character*

· Guide the story so that its major actions point in a single direction

Although each of us manifests all three *types of intent* in some aspect of his daily life, one *type of intent* tends to dominate his actions by default and to thereby define his basic nature. That nature may result from many factors, including his background, physical gifts and disabilities, pressing needs, age, and economic status—but the *type of intent* that describes it can provide important insight into what he is like at his most fundamental level.

By identifying a characteristic *type of intent* for the *main character*, the writer can guard against imposing inconsistent actions in the story and can provide clues regarding the strategies that the *main character* is likely to employ in any given situation. Such clues support the believability of the story and can be used to foreshadow its events.

Even if the *main character* is not readily definable by a characteristic *type of intent*, her primary actions will often align so that they represent a common *type of intent*. If her overall *intent* in the story involves a *gain* action, for example, her related actions and side stories will often also constitute *gain* actions. Likewise, if her main *intent* involves *keeping*, her related actions may represent *keep* actions.

These principles are well illustrated by three stories the *main characters* of which exhibit the three different *types of intent*:

+ *Rocky*—Rocky Balboa (*gain*)
+ *The Fugitive*—Richard Kimble (*regain*)
+ *A Christmas Carol*—Ebenezer Scrooge (*keep*)

## Rocky—Rocky Balboa (Gain)

In the film *Rocky*, the *main character*, Rocky Balboa, is a small-time boxer with a mixed-results fighting record who works as a debt collector for a Philadelphia loan shark. When the current heavyweight champion, Apollo Creed, finds himself without an opponent for an upcoming match, he decides to give a chance to an unknown fighter as a way of connecting the fight promotion to the U.S. Bicentennial celebration and invoking the idea that America is the "land of opportunity." After examining the list of available candidates, he chooses Rocky.

Rocky accepts the challenge, not only because it allows him to stand in the ring with a great boxer whose skills he truly admires but because it presents him with the opportunity to *gain* a *treasure* that he has never before possessed—a sense of deserved respect. As he remarks privately on the evening before the fight, he does not hope to win the boxing match; he simply hopes only to do what no boxer before him has done—to last the entire 15 rounds against Apollo without being knocked out. These personal stakes at the core of his story are what make it engaging and infuse it with power. He is not a brash young man *attempting* to achieve glory for its own sake; he is a humble young man *attempting* to feel good about himself.

From the moment that Rocky appears at the news conference announcing the fight, he engages in efforts most of which are aligned with his *type of intent* as a *gain* character. When he exercises to prepare his body for the fight, for example, it is not to return to a state of health that he enjoyed previously and lost; it is to attain a level of physical conditioning that he has never known before, so that he will be in the best shape of his life to meet the challenge of fighting Apollo Creed. Likewise, the knowledge about boxing that he *gains* from his trainer, Mickey, provides a necessary enrichment of his skills.

His side stories, too, are filled with *gain* efforts—for example, in his romantic pursuit of the shy young pet-store employee, Adrian. Her affection for him is a *treasure* that he does not possess at the start of the story, and his *attempts* to attain it—for example, by telling jokes or taking her ice skating—constitute *gain* efforts. And when he acquires her affection, he not only *gains* a specific *treasure* that he intentionally sought; he renders himself stronger emotionally and better prepared for battle.

Although Rocky does not seem to possess a *type of intent* that characterizes an overarching set of drives in his life, the efforts that he demonstrates throughout the story are those of a *gain* character, and most of his actions are aligned with that *type of intent*. And even though his ultimate effort involves a *keep intent*, to withstand the blows of the reigning champion for 15 rounds, it is performed in service to his overarching *intent* to *gain* a sense of deserved respect.

## The Fugitive—Richard Kimble (Regain)

In the film *The Fugitive*, Chicago vascular surgeon Dr. Richard Kimble is unjustly convicted of murdering his wife and is sentenced to death by lethal injection. On the way to the penitentiary in the prison bus, his fellow convicts mount a violent escape attempt, which results in his accidental freedom. After fleeing the scene and avoiding recapture, he returns to Chicago to discover and expose the truth behind his wife's murder so that he can clear his name and bring the true perpetrator to justice. To do so, he must evade capture by a deputy U.S. marshal while performing his own private investigation into the crime.

Richard's quest to clear his name is driven by a *regain intent* wherein the *treasure* that he no longer possesses is his reputation as a good and moral man who would not kill his wife. When he finds himself confronted by the deputy marshal shortly after his escape, he invokes his innocence to justify maintaining his freedom and is promptly informed that the invocation is insufficient to its purpose. If he hopes to restore his reputation, he will need to escape yet again and pursue the restoration on his own. Which he does.

In this case, the *regain intent* of the *main character* is entirely consistent with his characteristic *type of intent* as a surgeon whose profession calls on him to restore the health of his patients. Both efforts involve the *regaining* of a *treasure* that has been lost, taken away, or destroyed. If he were a cosmetic surgeon who specialized in nose jobs, his characteristic *intent* would lie in the realm of *gaining*—specifically, the improvement of his patients' faces. And the story would be affected accordingly.

As with most complex stories, *The Fugitive* involves a hearty mix of all three *types of intent*. Some of Richard's actions involve *keeping*—for example, disguising himself to *keep* hidden his identity and performing a death-defying jump from a dam to *keep* his freedom. Others involve *gaining*, such as acquiring knowledge about artificial limbs and searching hospital records in an attempt to identify the one-armed man whom he knows to be the killer. In fact, *gaining* may be said to lie at the very heart of the investigation that serves as his central effort in the story. In this case, however, he exerts the *gain* effort in pursuit of the greater goal of clearing his name, which is a *regain intent*.

In the end, he *succeeds* in his *attempt* to identify and expose those who are responsible for the crime and thereby clears his name. We-the-audience are *pleased* that he does so, and the credits roll.

## A Christmas Carol—Ebenezer Scrooge (Keep)

In Charles Dickens' classic story, *A Christmas Carol*, the *main character*, Ebenezer Scrooge, is a wealthy miser. There are many ways for rich men to behave—some spend freely; others seem always to be searching for new ways to increase their holdings. But Scrooge is neither of those. Scrooge is a tightwad. He maintains a very close eye on the money he has and is reticent to part with it for even his own basic needs, much less those of others. As Dickens describes him: "Oh! But he was a tight-fisted hand at the grind-stone... Hard and sharp as a flint, from which no steel had ever struck out generous fire, secret, and self-contained, and solitary as an oyster."

When it comes to money, Ebenezer Scrooge is a *keep* character—and his *intent* with regard to money is to *keep* what he has, not to go betting the house for more. In this respect, he presents a stark contrast to Gordon Gekko, the power hungry corporate raider from the film *Wall Street*, who is all about *gaining* (and who is not the *main character* in that story).

In the context of *A Christmas Carol*, *keeping* is what Scrooge is about. And at the beginning of the story, he is satisfied with his world as it exists. Notice, I did not say that he is happy, only that he is content enough with the condition of his world that he sees no need to take action to change it. Again, Dickens writes: "It was the very thing he liked. To edge his way along the crowded paths of life, warning all human sympathy to keep its distance..." We-the-audience might find the value of that satisfaction lacking, but at the beginning of the story Scrooge possesses a *treasure* that he values very much—a comfortable isolation and miserliness. And if left to himself, that condition would likely continue to exist until he died a lonely old man.

The problem for Scrooge, of course, is that Dickens does not leave him to himself. He visits him with four ghostly agents of change. The resulting tag-team fight is between Scrooge, whose *intent* is to *keep* the miserliness he values, and the ghosts, who spend the night attacking his world view and attempting to tear down the walls of selfishness that he has spent many years constructing.

Scrooge is a *keep* character. His *intent* is to *keep* his world as it is—to survive the attacks of the ghosts and to wake in the morning unchanged. And because his miserliness is a *keep* characteristic, his *type of intent* in the story is consistent with his general nature. If Dickens had imbued him with an insatiable captain-of-industry lust for financial conquest, the story would change entirely, not only in its particulars but in the *goals* of both Scrooge and the ghosts. Because he did not do so, however, *A Christmas Carol* is devoid of actions that seem false or contrived.

Oh, and by the way: Does Scrooge *succeed* or *fail* in the *goal* of his *intent*—that is, to *keep* his miserly world intact against the assault of the ghosts? If you haven't read or seen the story, forgive me for ruining the ending, but he *fails* completely and utterly.* Does he end up happier for having *failed*? Absolutely. And are we-the-audience glad for him? For those of us who advocate generosity of spirit, the answer is most definitely "yes." So here is a story in which the *main character fails* to achieve his story *goal*, and we-the-audience reckon his *failure* to be a positive *outcome*.

How very curious. Perhaps it merits further exploration in Part Two.

## CONSTRUCTION OF THE STORY

In addition to providing significant insights into the *main character*, the *grok approach* can be used to explore and develop the structural details of the story. In particular, it is useful for addressing the following matters.

- Revealing the time frame of concern
- Defining progress in the story
- Signaling points of structural reference
- Unearthing commonalities between stories
- Identifying characteristic *types of intent*
- Identifying the *treasure*
- Revealing strategies and tactics

And because the *main character* does most of the heavy lifting in the telling, it is impossible to approach such matters without appealing directly to her *intent*. It is this symbiosis between the *intent* of the *main character* and the story structure that renders the *grok approach* a powerful and integrated method for thinking about and working with stories.

---

* In Dickens' original version of the tale, Scrooge's initial resistance to the ghosts dissolves pretty quickly, which makes the second act seem a bit long and perhaps unnecessarily cruel to its *main character*, who gives up without much of a fight.

## REVEALING THE TIME FRAME OF CONCERN

Every story has a time frame of concern—that is, a general era (past, present, or future) that serves as the primary focus for the efforts and attention of the *main character*. As it happens, the time frame of concern is directly related to the *type of intent* that drives the story. Basically, it works like this.

- A *gain* character is focused on the future.
- A *regain* character is focused on the past.
- A *keep* character is focused on the present.

A research scientist who spends long nights in the laboratory searching for (*intending* to *gain*) the unknown cure for a deadly disease is focused on the moment of discovery in the future when her efforts might finally pay off. A man who returns to the town of his youth intent on restoring (*regaining*) the honor of his family is focused on the past—specifically the era that defined the family honor and the events that led to its loss. A woman trapped in a building and *attempting* to stay (*keep*) alive against the efforts of bloodthirsty hooligans who pursue her is focused on the frightening present and the immediate threat to her well-being.

By revealing the time frame of concern for the story, the *grok approach* helps the writer focus on those time-related matters that best serve its telling and avoid having it drift off into regions that constitute distractions. For example, the past is important to the man who seeks to restore his family honor, because that is where the origins of his *treasure* lie. Consequently, it is appropriate for the writer to incorporate memories and flashbacks in the story, because they color and inform it. For the woman trapped in the building, however, memories and flashbacks are unimportant except insofar as they help her to accomplish her objective of staying alive. So even if they are included in the story, their purposes differ from those of the returning son. Whereas his might be melancholic, hers are likely to be focused on recalling information that allows her to achieve her immediate *goal* of surviving. By the same token, she is not likely to spend time imagining a future free of the hooligans, because her attention is focused on staying alive long enough to witness such a future if it comes.

## DEFINING PROGRESS IN THE STORY

As I noted in Chapter 2, the sense of progress in any story is defined in reference to the *main character* and her *goal*. When expressed in terms of the *grok approach*, it may be said to depend on the specifics of her *intent* and *treasure*. Consequently, by clearly identifying the *intent* and *treasure* for the *main character*, the writer provides his audience with a concrete means of gauging story progress.

Imagine for a moment that you are in the middle of a featureless desert under a scorching midday sun, walking toward a distant X-marks-the-spot location upon which stands a tall obelisk. At any given moment in your journey, you can determine your progress by looking at the obelisk. If it seems to get larger, you are probably moving toward it. If it seems to get smaller, you are likely moving away. And if it seems to remain the same size, you have either stopped moving or are somehow circling around it.

Imagine now that the obelisk disappears—suddenly, in a flash, as if by magic. Does it become more difficult to gauge your progress toward the X-marked spot? Absolutely. Why? Because you no longer possess a clear means of determining your location with respect to the spot. The desert is featureless, remember, and even if you can look to your immediate surroundings for clues that you are moving, they provide no measure of progress toward your goal. Consequently, you might as well be standing still.

Purposeless movement and stasis are the enemies of poetic faith. By providing a clear indicator of where the story is headed—as embodied in the *intent* of the *main character* to *gain*, *regain*, or *keep* a *treasure*—you give us-the-audience a map, as if to say, "Here's where we're headed. Why not tag along and see if we make it?" And yes, we appreciate that.

## SIGNALING POINTS OF STRUCTURAL REFERENCE

Well-told stories often contain intuitive points of reference that let the audience know where it is in relation to the structure of the story—that is, whether it is nearer the beginning, middle, or end. Such points do not proclaim themselves with bright, flashing lights and blow their whistles like traffic cops as the audience passes their checkpoints. Instead, they advise the audience like friendly tour guides, saying, "That's all there is to see in the kitchen. Let's head upstairs." And by so doing, they keep the story moving and the audience grounded with a sense of location.

Such points of structural reference typically divide the story into three acts—traditionally referred to as Act I, Act II, and Act III. And just as each part of a building contributes to its overall function, each act performs a distinct purpose in the story. Act I, for example, introduces us-the-audience to the story world and its inhabitants and lays the foundations for the journey that we will undertake in the vehicle of the *main character*. In this way, it may be said to create a travel brochure of the story world, including a map of its terrain and directions to the X-marked spot that serves as our measure of progress. Act II lets us experience the roughness of the terrain itself and usually leads to a metaphorical battlefield on which some ultimate decision will be made, some irreversible course will be taken, or some final conflict will be played out. Act III hands us field passes for the battlefield sideline, allows us to experience the battle first-hand, and lets us know where things stand when the smoke clears.

If a story is built on a firm structural foundation, it may function seamlessly, and the acts themselves will transition invisibly from one to the other as the story progresses. If the structure is shaky, however, the audience may feel unsettled and edgy, sensing that something is wrong but not knowing what.

Many years ago, I went with a friend to a second-run theatre to see *Mad Max*, a low-budget Australian film that few realized would launch the career of Mel Gibson as a Hollywood superstar. And although I found the movie to be mildly entertaining, I remember feeling a sense of foundering as I watched it, as if I were making unsteady progress up the side of a sand dune and witnessing events that might or might not lead to some kind of dramatic conclusion. When, at last, the conclusion came, it arrived with surprising and unsatisfying swiftness. Then the credits rolled, the lights came up, and my friend and I went bowling, neither of us wowed by the film.

At the time, I had not yet cast off the mantle of engineering to serve the Gods of Fiction, but as a fan of the well-told story, and having seen many films that I considered brilliantly done, I knew that something was wrong. Some element of the storytelling was missing. And although I cannot honestly say that the search for that missing element has defined my life ever since, I can say that the experience stuck in my mind and bubbled to the surface whenever I thought of the film, and some small part of me would wonder: What was wrong with *Mad Max*?

If I had been aware of the tenets of the *grok approach* at the time, the answer would have been obvious—Act I is way too long. Simply put, it takes Max the better part of the movie to get mad. The bulk of the film serves as nothing more than a set up to the final conflict, and when the final conflict arrives, it lacks the emotional power it could have had if the story had been properly structured. The film, in a sense, is a giant first act with a second act tacked on at the end to segue to the credits.

In a well-told story, the audience is not rationally aware of the divisions between acts; it simply feels them as shifts in the focus of its attention and senses them as hidden signposts along the story path, as I did in *Mad Max*. The writer, on the other hand, must be conscious not only of their presence but of their whereabouts, in the same way that an architect knows the layout of a building, so that he can ensure its structural integrity even as he conceals the details of its construction. In this respect, the *grok approach* is especially useful, because it provides important clues regarding the locations of major structural points in any story—two in particular:

• End of Act I

• End of the story

## End of Act I

The end of Act I is important in any story, because it is the point at which all of the significant groundwork has been laid, including the "Will she or won't she *succeed?*" question that needs to be answered in the mind of the audience. As important as this signpost is, however, writers are often confused regarding where to find it in their own works, especially first drafts of works-in-progress. The *grok approach* is singularly helpful in this regard, because it identifies the story *goal* and thereby provides a concrete definition for the end of Act I—specifically:

> Act I is over when the audience knows who the *main character* is, what she *intends* to accomplish in the story, and why she possesses the *intent*.

These three elements—*main character*, *intent*, and purpose behind the *intent*—comprise answers to the fundamental questions regarding the *who*, *what*, *why* of the story. When they are combined with the *where*-and-*when* context of the story, which is also laid out in Act I, they leave only one thing to be determined—the *how* that plays out in Acts II and III.

In this sense, Act I can be thought of as simply "the tale of how the *main character* comes to possess her *intent*." And because the *treasure* is the focus of the *intent*, this definition provides the story *goal* that we-the-audience will use to measure progress.

In *A Christmas Carol*, we open on a 19th-century London counting house on a bitingly cold Christmas Eve, where we meet a grouchy old businessman and learn of his miserly ways. We witness his exchanges with an employee he keeps under his thumb, two men who have come to entreat him for a charitable donation, and his cheery nephew—all of which reinforce the picture of this man as a stingy grump. The businessman is our *main character*, and he lives in a compassionless world of his own making.

That night, alone in his house, he hears a steady stream of frightening noises and suddenly finds the ghost of his long-dead business partner coming through the doors of his bedroom—a ghost who is condemned to walk the earth in chains because of his own lack of compassion when he was alive. The ghost informs him that he will soon be haunted by three other spirits without whose visits "you cannot hope to shun the path I tread." Then the ghost goes to the window and floats out into the night to join a chorus of forlorn phantoms like himself.

At this point in the story, we know the identity of the *main character* (Ebenezer Scrooge), what he *intends* (to maintain his world view against spirits who will pressure him to change his compassionless ways), and why (because they are coming for him, and he has no choice but to engage).

End of Act I.

In the film *Blade Runner*, we open on a futuristic vision of Los Angeles, a dark and rainy world with smoky interiors reminiscent of the 1940s but with cooler technology. We meet a former cop on a rain-soaked street and follow him to a sidewalk café, where he is accosted mid-bite by an emissary from his one-time supervisor who is calling him in for a job. We meet the supervisor and learn the situation—four renegade androids are walking the streets of Los Angeles. The former cop is offered the chance to hunt them down and kill them. When he refuses, he is threatened into compliance. If he *wants* to remain free to live his life as he pleases, he has no choice.

We know the identity of the *main character* (Rick Deckard), what he *intends* (to find and terminate the renegade androids), and why (because the assignment is forced upon him).

Cue the music for Act II.

In the film *Back to the Future*, we find ourselves in a small California town, circa 1985, where a high school student whose family life is far from ideal befriends a slightly mad scientist who has succeeded in inventing a time machine. In the process of befriending the scientist, the student is thrown thirty years into the past, where his very presence threatens to derail the boy-girl relationship that will result in his own birth. To restore the timeline of his life to its former balance and make sure that he and his siblings are born, he must repair the damaged relationship and get back to his own era before the chance to do so passes him by.

We know who is the *main character* (Marty McFly), what he *intends* (to return to his proper place in time and undo any damage his displacement has brought about in the meantime), and why (because his very life is at stake).

Pass the popcorn and shhhh! Act II is about to start.

In each of these cases, Act I can be thought of simply as the tale of how the *main character* comes to possess the *intent* that drives the story. The manner in which the act plays out may vary widely from story to story, but the principle holds in every case. And when you think of Act I in these terms, it becomes a whole lot easier to create.

## Genesis of the Intent

One handy aspect of the *grok approach* is that it clears up a potential point of confusion regarding the genesis of the *intent* that propels the story. Specifically, it highlights the fact that the *intent* of the *main character* does not necessarily exist at the beginning of the story and is, in fact, usually generated somewhere in Act I.

When a beginning writer considers the old saw concerning what his character *wants*, it is easy (and deceptive) to think in terms of the *main character* possessing her desire and *intent* from the outset of the story—

almost as if she were born with them and has had them for years by the time we-the-audience first meet her. But that is not how desires and *intents* work in real life, and neither do they work that way in a well-told story. It is true that a character may possess a general *intent* by the time we meet her, but general *intents* do not drive stories. Each story is driven by the specific *intent* of its *main character*, and that specific *intent* arises from a specific desire on the part of the *main character* and the specific opportunity or requirement to fulfill that desire.

So in defining Act I as "the tale of how the *main character* comes to possess her *intent*," we can add "an *intent* that she might or might not possess at the start of the story"—when the lights rise on stage or we crack open the cover to page one.

Do you want to write an effective first act? Introduce us-the-audience to the *main character* and her story world and illustrate the circumstances and sequence of events that generate her *intent*. Make clear to us her *treasure* and *goal* and how we are to measure her *success* or *failure*. Then go feed the cat, get some coffee, come back, sit down, and start writing Act II.

## Dependence on the Audience

Not only does the *grok approach* clarify matters regarding the genesis of *intent*, it reveals a critical fact about the structure of Act I—that the end of the act is defined in terms of the audience rather than any character in the story, even the *main character*. That is to say, it does not matter when the *main character* becomes aware of her *intent*; what matters with respect to the structure of Act I is when the *audience* becomes aware of that *intent*.

It is entirely possible, for example, to create a story in which the *main character* already possesses her *intent* by the time we-the-audience meet her. In that case, we enter the story as if we were being lowered from a helicopter onto the top of a moving train. But just because the action is already in progress by the time we arrive does not mean that the story cannot have a first act. It means, rather, that we must be provided a steady stream of clues regarding the identity of the *main character* and her *intent* as we race toward the first major encounter in the story.

Regardless of whether the story opens at rest or full speed, the end of Act I is defined by the awareness of the audience regarding the *who* and *why* of the story—*not* by that awareness on the part of the *main character*.

## End of the Story

In addition to simplifying the concept of Act I in any story, the *grok approach* provides a straightforward means of ensuring that the story ends at a proper point. Upon first hearing, of course, the matter sounds absurd. After all, stories end when the lights come up and the credits roll or the last word of the novel has been read. Don't they?

Not by law, no. They may *stop* at that point, but they *end* there only if the writer knows what he is doing and is respectful of his audience.

By definition, the writer reigns as Story God in any work of his creation. Consequently, he has the divine right to stop the story wherever he damn well pleases—even in mid-sentence if he likes. Doing so is usually a bad idea, however, because it leaves the audience unsatisfied and, in some cases, downright resentful. The audience member buys a ticket to go all the way to the terminal station, not to be dumped in the weeds at the side of the tracks outside of town.

This does not mean that everything needs to be neatly wrapped up by the time the credits roll. It means only that the journey of the *main character* should come to a definite conclusion, even if that conclusion involves her realization that the *goal* she seeks is forever beyond her reach.

Just as it is important to know where the story begins and to lay its groundwork efficiently, so it is important to know where it ends and to see that it lands with dramatic grace. And here, the *grok approach* provides clear guidance, because it dictates when the journey is complete. Specifically, it decrees that:

> The story cannot end until the audience receives clear indication of whether the *main character* has *succeeded* or *failed* in her quest to satisfy her *intent*.

The detective will discover the identity of the murderer before he slips into oblivion... or not. The boy will win the heart of the girl before she says "I do" to someone else... or not. The king will defeat the assaulting horde before it breaches the castle walls... or not.

And here the *grok approach* provides unique insight, as well—because it reveals how the *outcome* must relate to the *type of intent*. A *gain* story cannot end, for example, until the *main character* either *succeeds* in *gaining* the *treasure* or *fails* in a manner that makes the *gaining* moot—for example, by running out of time or options. A *regain* story cannot end until the *main character* either *succeeds* in *regaining* her *treasure* or *fails* in a manner that makes the *regaining* impossible—for example, because the loved one whose health she hoped to restore passes away. And a *keep* story is not over until either the *treasure* is lost or the threat to its possession is utterly vanquished.

In each case, the story is not concluded satisfactorily until the *succeed/ fail outcome* is known to the audience. And the *outcome* must contain a sense of finality. It must take the form of the job opportunity that will never return, the murderer who vanishes into oblivion, the attacking horde so utterly defeated that it can never again mount an assault. It is reasonable to assert, in fact, that the *grok approach* informs the writer regarding one of the most important aspects of a well-told story—the satisfying *outcome*.

## UNEARTHING COMMONALITIES BETWEEN STORIES

Because the *grok approach* applies to every story regardless of its genre, form, or medium, it can be used to reveal commonalities between stories that may appear at first glance to be completely unrelated. Such commonalities can be used, in turn, to inform the story creation process, especially with respect to the strategies used by characters to accomplish their goals.

The young man seeking the attentions of a girl is just as much of a *gain* character as the research scientist who spends long nights in the laboratory to discover a cure for cancer. And both share the *gain* characteristic with the woman *attempting* to *gain* a sense of acceptance from her father.

The hobbit on a journey to return a magic ring to its fiery birthplace is just as much of a *regain* character as a young man displaced in time who struggles to return to his proper era. And both share the *regain* characteristic with the native chieftain who leads his tribe to retake dominion of his ancestral lands from an invasive group of settlers.

The woman trapped in the building and *attempting* to stay alive is just as much of a *keep* character as the compassionless London businessman who *attempts* to maintain his miserliness against the efforts of spirits who entreat him to change. And both share the *keep* characteristic with the deep-cover spy who *attempts* to hide his true identity from nosey neighbors.

Different genres, characters, settings, eras, and backstories, and yet... the same three *types of intent*.

We watch the television show to find out if the detective will *succeed* or *fail* in his *attempt* to *gain* the identity of the killer. We view the film to find out if the boy will *succeed* or *fail* in his *attempt* to return to (*regain* his place within) his proper era. We read the novella to find out if the businessman will *succeed* or *fail* in his *attempt* to *keep* his miserliness intact. In short, we invest our attention in any story to find out one thing primarily—whether the *main character* will *succeed* or *fail* in her *attempt* to *gain*, *regain*, or *keep* her *treasure*.

This ability of the *grok approach* to identify commonalities between disparate stories lies at the heart of the practice of *meta-adaptation*, which I describe in Part Three of this book. In brief, *meta-adaptation* involves using the *grok approach* to expose the throbbing innards of a story or idea and employ those innards to construct a new story from scratch. The story thus created may differ so completely from its adapted source that all of their common attributes seem to disappear completely, even to the writer. But if their *grok*-defined innards are identical, they may be rightly said to share the same genes.

The medieval king *attempting* to defend his castle from the attacking horde has more in common with the modern suburban mother trying to hold her family together than he does with the gallant knight who has committed himself to finding the Holy Grail. The king and the mother are *keep* characters, *attempting* to *keep* a *treasure* that is under threat of being lost. The knight is a *gain* character and has more in common with the 1940s private detective than he does with the king he left behind.

## IDENTIFYING CHARACTERISTIC TYPES OF INTENT

As I noted above, people in real life and characters in well-told stories tend to exhibit characteristic *types of intent* that define who they are and how they may behave in any given situation. Some characteristic *types of intent* derive from outside factors such as background, culture, and position in a relationship; others stem from inherent factors like gender or age. To understand the effect of such factors, it is instructive to look at five of the most influential:

• Inherent nature
• Age
• Position in a relationship
• Occupation
• Story role

## Inherent Nature

Most of us at some point in our lives have encountered people who, seemingly from birth, have set their sights on "getting theirs"—achieving, acquiring, and grappling with all comers to make sure that their needs are satisfied. We might not like or trust such people. We might consider them threats to the well-being of society and build prisons to accommodate those who pursue their *intents* by means we deem inappropriate. We might raise armies to fight them when they threaten the security of nations. Or we might admire their unwillingness to be denied satisfaction and elevate them to positions of power in the hope that they will fight for our principles.

Most of us have also met people who value cooperation over conflict and whose *intents* have less to do with getting than they do with peace-keeping—and who are willing to sacrifice their own needs to maintain harmony within a family, group, or community. We tend to trust such people more than we do the getters, because they seem, at least on the surface, to have in mind the good of the collective. Then again, we might not place them in positions of power, simply because politics sometimes requires conflict that they might seek to avoid, thereby fumbling the ball of our best interests in the process.

In these two cases, the getters and peacekeepers can be generally described as *gain* and *keep* characters, respectively. This does not mean that one is aggressive and the other is docile—some *gain* characters use passive-aggressive faux-docility to get what they want, and some *keep* characters fight tooth and nail to protect the peace they are maintaining. But with regard to their characteristic *types of intent* and the actions that stem from them, getters *gain* and peacekeepers *keep*.

This ability of the *grok approach* to identify the characteristic *type of intent* for any character can prove profoundly useful when creating a story. In fact, it far outshines the common storytelling exercise of creating a complete dossier for each character, as if one were running a background check for the CIA. Habits, rearing, and preferences matter, to be sure, but their importance pales in comparison to the underlying nature of the characters with respect to their *types of intent*.

If I create a story about a nurse who is strapped for cash and driven to filching drugs from work and selling them on the street, I do not need to know what color lipstick she uses, whether she won a spelling bee in high school, or how she takes her eggs at breakfast. If at some point she walks into a diner and orders eggs, I'll deal with it then... and will be surprised if it makes one iota of difference. To waste time concerning myself with whether she likes them sunny side up or soft-boiled before I start creating the story is to commit a crime against the Gods of Fiction.*

What I do need to know is *why* my nurse needs the money. Is it to pay the rent so that her family is not thrown out of their apartment? Is it to support another kind of addiction she possesses? Is it to post bail for her brother? Does she feel compelled to buy a pair of fashionable shoes?

Screw how she takes her eggs! I need to know her *intent*!

## Age

It should not be surprising that age plays a role in determining the characteristic *type of intent* for any character. After all, with advancement in age comes changes in health, ability, and need.

Young people, for example, often exhibit *gain intents*, because they are at the times in their lives when they are engaged in the matter of accumulation—seeking knowledge, taking on new jobs, buying property, and acquiring friends who may help them achieve their life goals. They may also exhibit *keep* characteristics wherein the *treasure* that they currently possess is the freedom to live life as they like. Older people, on the other hand, tend to

---

* The same idea holds for character quirks. If you have ever received the advice that to enhance one of your characters you should grant her an interesting quirk, let me recommend something: *Ignore it with extreme prejudice.* Slap on the earphones and crank up the music until the vibrations drive the advice out of your skull. Then call your lawyer to get a restraining order against whoever gave you the advice. They're hurting you, and it's time to move on.

manifest *intents* related to *keeping*—for example, maintaining possession of their bank accounts, homes, or health. They may also have *intents* related to *regaining* abstract *treasures* such as love or lost vitality.

This fundamental relationship between age and characteristic *type of intent* may explain, in part, the dearth of popular stories involving older *main characters*—especially women. Any culture that glorifies "getting" will naturally promote stories that involve *gain* characters. And since older characters are prone to exhibit *keep* or *regain types of intent*, they are excluded from consideration at the outset.

## Position in a Relationship

Many characteristic *types of intent* can be correlated to positions and roles in relationships. A mother, for example, might try to *keep* her family together against the efforts of her disgruntled son to tear it apart (to *gain* its destruction). Likewise, a young woman might try to *gain* the affections of a wealthy married man, hoping to usurp the position of his current wife and thereby to *gain* a life of luxury that she has never known. The wife, on the other hand, as current owner of the wedding ring, might strive to *keep* the marriage intact and might employ any number of tactics to do so, including the murder of the would-be mistress.

## Occupation

Occupations, too, may be associated with characteristic *types of intent*. For example, investigation of any sort is a *gain* activity; therefore, a detective of any kind is likely to exhibit *gain* characteristics. A public librarian, on the other hand, is likely to manifest *keep* characteristics, maintaining the local archive of knowledge. And a restorer in any field is involved in a *regain* activity.

Even within a profession, however, specialization can give rise to different *types of intent*. A research physician, for example, is a *gain* character whose *intent* is to discover and reveal medical truths and, thereby, *gain* new medical knowledge. An old country doctor, on the other hand, is likely to exhibit *keep* characteristics, performing his duties to maintain the health of those under his care. And a physician specializing in physical rehabilitation is a *regain* character who helps her patients restore the use of their limbs.

It is impossible to list here every walk of life and its associated characteristic *type of intent*. (But a collection is well worth compiling.) The point is simply that occupations, paid or otherwise, tend to be associated with specific *types of intent*. And the savvy writer can make use of this fact when creating his story, either by using an occupation to reinforce the characteristics of the *main character* or "playing against type" by creating a *main character* whose *type of intent* in the story contrasts that of her job.

## Story Role

In addition to identifying the *type of intent* of the *main character*, the *grok approach* helps identify the *intent* of the opposing character* or force. For example, if a *main character intends* to *gain* possession of a valuable jewel, she might be opposed by a *keep* character who currently possesses the jewel or by another *gain* character who *intends* to acquire it for her own. If she is successful in her efforts, the character who previously possessed the jewel might *intend* to *regain* possession, in which case the *main character* must engage in *keeping* the jewel she *succeeded* in *gaining*.

In most cases, a *gain* character is opposed by a *keep* character, a *regain* character, or another *gain* character. Likewise, a *regain* character faces off against a *keep* character, *gain* character, or another *regain* character whose ownership of the *treasure* goes farther back in time. A *keep* character, on the other hand, is opposed typically by a *gain* character or *regain* character, not by another *keep* character—for the simple reason that two *keep* characters are satisfied with their respective *treasures*, and neither is likely to threaten the other or rock the boat.

### IDENTIFYING THE TREASURE

*Treasures* come in many different flavors and forms. Some can be experienced through the five senses—for example, a necklace, an embarrassing photograph, or the key to a hidden safe. Others are abstract, such as the affection of a love interest, the health of a loved one, or a position of honor or power. And they can be generally grouped into three main categories: physical, psychological, and spiritual. Physical *treasures* are those that are tangible, whether abstract or not, such as an object, control of a piece of property, or victory in a contest. Psychological *treasures* are associated with feelings, such as a sense of acceptance by a group or the feeling of being loved. Spiritual *treasures* are internal to the character who attains them, such as a sense of inner peace.

Categorizations such as these are not always cut and dried. In many cases, for example, a physical *treasure* serves as merely a *trophy* to invoke a feeling, and it is the feeling itself that constitutes the actual *treasure*. It is the ability of the *grok approach* to reveal such distinctions that allows the writer to probe the depths of his *main character* and discover the *treasure* that will satisfy her desire and generate her true *intent*.

Regardless of the nature of the *treasure*, the writer must provide the audience with an explicit means of determining whether the *main character*

---

* I use the term "opposing character" here rather than "antagonist," because the force or entity that prevents the *main character* from accomplishing her goal is not necessarily antagonistic to her. In some stories, in fact, Nature itself is the opposing character and cannot be said to be antagonistic to the *main character*. It applies its laws and forces without prejudice.

*succeeds* or *fails* in her *attempt* to pursue it. For the woman locked in the building with bloodthirsty hooligans, for example, the indicator can be simply stated as "staying alive until the hooligans either give up or are driven away." For the father seeking a cure for a life-threatening disease that ails his son, the indicator is "finding a cure for the son before the disease wins out."

Even abstract *treasures* require concrete means of measurement to be useful in a story. The boy stuck thirty years in the past will either show up again in his own era... or he won't. The miserly businessman will either display a change in behavior... or he won't. The jaded night club owner will either let down his guard and re-enter the world of those who actively get involved in the lives of others... or he won't.

In short, the writer must make sure to answer in clear terms the basic question that the audience will ask regarding the *success* or *failure* of the *main character*—that is: How will we know?

## REVEALING STRATEGIES AND TACTICS

All *intended* actions involve strategies and tactics that are used in the *attempt* to achieve specific *goals*. Because the *grok approach* focuses on the *intent* of the *main character*, it allows the writer to examine her strategies and tactics and to draw parallels with those used by characters in other stories who share her *type of intent*.

As an example of such parallels and their usefulness, consider an army general *attempting* to *gain* control of a well-defended hill and a boy *attempting* to *gain* the affections of a girl at school. As a first try, both might try a direct assault—the general charging the hill with guns blazing, the boy stepping up bravely to the girl to introduce himself and ask her to dance. And both tactics might fail, causing the *main character* in each case to go back to the drawing board and find another way to achieve his *goal*.

As a second try, the general might decide to probe the enemy defenses for signs of weakness—and the boy might study the girl to learn what she likes. The general might find an undefended pass; the boy might discover that the girl has a soft spot for puppies—and each might try to use the information to his advantage. Or perhaps the general decides that he and his troops do not have the firepower to capture the hill on their own. In that case, he might seek an ally. Likewise, the love-struck boy might seek the help of a friend whom the girl trusts and induce the friend to speak well of him in her presence.

So even though one of our *main characters* is involved in armed conflict and the other is dealing with issues of the heart (hopefully not involving weapons), both are employing identical strategies and tactics. Only the details differ.

If we turn our examples around now and view them through the eyes of the opposing characters—the renegade leader defending the hill and the girl whose affections the boy seeks—we discover a different set of common strategies and tactics. And in this case the commonalities stem from the fact that both opposing characters are engaged in *keep* actions. Each character might, for example, call on allies of his or her own. The renegade leader might implore nearby villagers to come to his aid by fighting the general and his army before they can take the hill. The girl might ask her older brother to threaten the boy. Or either might feign surrender in hopes of luring his or her opposing character into a trap.

In each of these cases, the strategies and tactics available to each character depend on, and may be limited by, his or her *type of intent*. The general, for example, can attack the hill until his supplies and troops are exhausted, try to exploit weaknesses in the enemy defenses, enlist the help of allies, employ new technology, lay siege to the hill until the renegades run out of food and water... or give up the fight, call off his troops, and go home. The renegade leader, on the other hand, may fend off the attacks as they come, enlist allies from the nearby village, employ new technology, mount an attack of his own, put up the white flag and surrender, or commit himself and his troops to Masada-like mass suicide.

Or—and this is important—he can make peace. His *intent*, after all, is to *keep* control of the hill. To do so, he must either hold out until the enemy gives up, defeat or neutralize the enemy; or somehow transform the enemy into a friend or neutral party. Of these three strategies, the third involves the least effort and resources and yet constitutes the most permanent solution. It is one thing to disable an opponent, leaving open the chance that he will recover and threaten again; it is another thing to transform him into an ally and thereby remove his motivation to attack. Both strategies accomplish the same *goal*; but the latter does so efficiently and without bloodshed.

Therein lies a lesson for life.

# Chapter 6

## APPLYING THE *grok* APPROACH

Like any good all-in-one tool, the *grok approach* has at least 1,001 uses. It won't open wine bottles or file your fingernails, but it does contain a reliable compass with which to navigate any story world and a razor-sharp machete to cut through the tangled underbrush of ideas that can sometimes grow up during the development of a story and threaten to choke it to death. And as with any useful tool, its expert application requires the deftness that comes with experience, but its basic functionality can be employed by any able-minded beginner.

This chapter serves as an introductory guide to using the *grok approach*. Its purpose is to describe and illustrate how to apply the approach when developing a story—not to review its complete functionality but to outline its most practical applications and provide instruction regarding their use.

Because the many aspects of the *grok approach* are intimately related to each other, they cannot be addressed in a completely modular fashion. To identify the *main character*, for example, the writer must use a *treasure* that stops the story. But to do so, he must find the *treasure* that best describes her *goal*. Is it marital union with the man of her dreams? Or is it the status that she will attain by means of the marriage? Is it the jewel she hopes to steal? Or is it the operation she hopes to pay for by selling the stolen jewel? And the *treasure* itself is of utmost importance for determining the *grok* type for the *main character*—that is, whether her *intent* lies in the realm of *gaining*, *regaining*, or *keeping*.

Due to this fundamental interrelatedness, the application of the *grok approach* tends to be an iterative endeavor—not a blind, trial-and-error process but a step-by-step narrowing of possibilities that leads to story truth. So no, it is not a modular process, but y'know what? It's modular enough. And we commit no sin by dividing the matter into essential tasks, the three most important of which are:

* Identifying the *main character*
* Determining the *type of intent*
* Examining the *treasure*

# IDENTIFYING THE MAIN CHARACTER

Every writer possesses his own unique approach to developing a story. Some go at the task methodically and try to imagine every detail of the story before plotting its course and turning the key that starts its engine. Others snatch the faintest of ideas and start creating, allowing the story to grow on its own however it will.

Both approaches have their perks and drawbacks. The first can generate a straightforward path to story completion but may lead to formulaic structures and the imposing of developments that feel false. The second avoids formulaic storytelling but may result in stories that are riddled with undisciplined chaos and multiple dead ends.

Regardless of approach, however, all writers face a fundamental task at some point in the process—identification of the *main character*. Whether she is identified at the outset of story creation or somewhere in the middle of the process, the writer must find and tag her clearly, so that the story can be properly developed and adjusted during its refinement.

Fortunately, the job of doing so does not involve sackcloth, fasting, or prayer. In fact, it can be accomplished by means of a simple thought experiment that relies on how a character feels when granted his *treasure* by unmerited grace.

## THE MAIN-CHARACTER THOUGHT EXPERIMENT

When I teach the full-length version of my course on the *grok approach*, I ask each student to bring to the first class a story that he is currently working on, regardless of its stage of development. During the get-to-know-you introductions, the students interview each other regarding their backgrounds and the stories they brought to class. In presentations that follow the interviews, we hear a thumbnail summary of each story, which helps to establish its baseline and allows me to gauge its development over the duration of the multi-session course.

The summaries are always revealing and usually provide jumping-off points that allow me to hint at basic concepts of the *grok approach*. My role in shepherding the process is largely twofold: a) to keep the summaries moving along, so that we do not end up mired in the bog of "so she rolls down the window and shouts obscenities at the nun" and b) to ensure that one fundamental question gets addressed in every case: Who is the *main character*? Even a cursory understanding of the *grok approach* makes clear why the question matters; every aspect of the story is touched by its answer.

In most cases, each student has a pretty good idea which character in his story fits the role of *main character*. Often, however, a student will have been struggling with that very question prior to coming to class, knowing intuitively that it must be answered but finding himself daunted by the task.

It also happens, on occasion, that the character who a student assumes to be his *main character* is, in fact, merely an active side character whose *intent* is not essential to the story.

This is where the *grok approach* first starts to glimmer, because it allows the writer to easily diagnose and remedy such situations by means of a simple thought experiment, the gist of which goes like this:

> To identify the *main character* in a story, don the mantle of Story God, all-powerful ruler of the story world, and search that world to find the one character for whom the magical granting of a single *treasure* will stop the story—not end it with a satisfying conclusion but bring it to a screeching halt.

Does a boy in your story long for the affections of a girl? Grant them to him magically—right now, before the story takes another step forward. Don't worry about the reasonability of doing so. You're Story God; magic is in your job description. When the boy possesses what he desires, gotten not through personal effort but simply by having it handed to him from on high, does the story lose its reason to go on? If the answer is "yes," the boy is your *main character*. If the answer is "no," keep looking, because the story really belongs to someone else—perhaps the girl, who might be protective of her affections.

Does your story involve a soldier in charge of defending an outpost from natives who are upset because it was built on sacred land? Frighten the natives into going away or visit the Angel of Death upon their village. Just somehow make them give up the fight, not with the idea of regrouping but forever. And not by virtue of anything the soldier might do but just because you, as Story God, say so. Does the story stop when the outpost is safe? The soldier in charge of its defense is your *main character*.

Is one of your characters a native chieftain *attempting* to destroy an outpost the presence of which dishonors sacred land? As Story God, let the ground open up and swallow the outpost. Send the Angel of Death to annihilate the ranks of its defenders. Play with the fabric of space-time and transport the whole thing to the other side of the universe. But render its disappearance a magical act having nothing to do with efforts on the part of the chieftain. When the outpost is gone, does the story stop? If so, the chieftain is your *main character*.

Remember, the thought experiment has one goal—to identify the *main character*. It is not meant to generate reasonable twists to incorporate into the story. When you grant the *treasure* that stops the story, you do not need to worry about how doing so will affect the story itself. In point of fact, it will not affect the story at all, because as soon as the granting has done its job by helping to identify the *main character*, it can be discarded.

To demonstrate the practical use of this experiment, let's look at an example scenario involving three primary characters any one of whom might serve as the *main character* in a story (but only one of whom does).

## THE PAINTER, THE BRIDE, AND HER HUSBAND

The thought experiment described above applies to any story regardless of its complexity or the size of its population. To illustrate its use and implications for story development, let's consider a story involving a torrid affair between an eccentric painter and the lovely young bride of a high-powered businessman. The question at hand is: Which one is the *main character*?

Is it the painter, whose interest in the bride may stem from her uncanny resemblance to a lover who vanished years before? By engaging in the affair, is he *attempting* to recapture the joy he felt with the lost love?

You're Story God. Wave your wand and grant what you guess might be his *treasure*. Un-lose the lost love. She was shipwrecked for years and only recently rescued by a tour boat. As soon as the boat reaches port, she races back to the painter. The doorbell rings, and there she is—sunburned, frazzled, missing a couple of teeth, but the jewel of his eye nonetheless. His heart leaps at the sight of her. She collapses into his arms. They're together again! His need to pursue the affair vanishes, leaving not so much as a puff of smoke. The painter is your *main character* and his pursuit of the feelings he possessed for the lost love is the measure that we-the-audience will use to gauge story progress. To develop the actual story, simply re-lose the lost love and concentrate again on the affair.

Or is the bride the *main character*? Perhaps, for example, she longs to be free from the stifling expectations of the society into which she has married. Maybe each time she and the painter make love, she feels powerful and defiant of that society, as if she is thrusting a middle finger into its face.

Pick up your Story God wand and point it right at her. Transport her into an alternate universe in which she never uttered the words "I do." Or bring another lover into her life—maybe someone of her station who shares her disdain for the toffee-nosed fuddy-duddies with whom they must both consort. Make him an indisputable trade-up from the painter. Then whisk them away to a tropical island where they can live out their days making love in a mosquito-netted featherbed while cool sea breezes waft in from the beach, wetting the sides of their ice-filled Mojito glasses—both of them content in their shared rejection of the society that sought to imprison them in its mores. Does the story stop and the affair end abruptly? If so, the bride is your *main character*, and it is her *attempt* to free herself from the bonds of upper-class stuffiness that we-the-audience will use to measure progress in the story and parse its *theme*.

Or does she have a gripe against her husband? Is he cruel to her, and is the affair her way of exacting revenge? Is she laying subtle clues to its discovery even as she entangles the painter with her wiles?

You're Story God—get rid of the husband. Don the black robe, stretch out a bony hand, and make him die. Be quick about it, and merciful if you like—a heart attack on the golf course or ill-timed step into traffic. Or bang him on the head and change his nature. Dislodge the tumor that has caused him to treat her badly. Let him apologize and pledge to make up for lost time. Does the story stop when the husband dies or becomes a new person? If so, the bride, again, is your *main character*. In this case, though, we-the-audience will gauge story progress by virtue of her efforts to punish her husband.

Or is she truly smitten with the painter? If she were to *gain* his love and lose all else, would she count herself blessed? So grant it, already—no questions asked. Fill up his heart with affection for her. Spirit them away to that tropical island with the mosquito-netted featherbed. Replace the Mojito glasses with flutes of Dom Perignon. Give them a trouble-free life filled with fresh fruit and afternoon lovemaking. Cue the sea breezes. Does the story stop? Once more, the bride is the *main character*. This time, however, it is her progress in acquiring the love of the painter that we-the-audience will look to for signs of progress in the story.

And keep in mind that your role in this exercise does not involve judging the *main character* with respect to her desires. The story will do that in the telling, and the audience will be sworn in as jurors the moment the story starts. Your job is simply to grant a *treasure* that stops the story, and your purpose in doing so is simply to identify the *main character*. To perform the experiment correctly, you must put your harrumphing on hold.

Or is the husband the *main character*? Did he marry his bride to climb a social ladder? And does the affair matter to him only because it threatens to knock out a rung? Get out your Story God stick and grant him the status he desires—securely and in a manner that cannot be affected by the affair. Does the story stop and the affair become unimportant? The husband is your *main character*, and his social standing is the *treasure* that will determine progress in the story.

Or is he truly in love with his bride? And is the possession of her love his *treasure*? To find out, grant it to him. End the affair abruptly. Fill her with genuine love for him, not in response to any action on his part but merely by virtue of undeserved grace from you as Story God. Send them to the feather-bedded island and wipe out the mosquitoes before they arrive. Does the story stop when her love is his? The husband is your *main character*, and progress in the story will be defined by the advances and retreats of his *attempt* to *gain* (or *regain*) the love of his wife.

Or is he concerned with something wholly within himself? Do the domineering tendencies that serve him well in the business world fill him with self-loathing when they hurt people for whom he cares? Does he long for a self-control he has never possessed? And when he finds out about the affair, does he look to change himself rather than attack the situation?

Mount the Story God throne and give him what he desires. Rewire his brain to bless him with self-restraint. Hit him with lightning or a sudden near-death experience that leaves him changed. Just make sure he emerges with the self-control he longs for. When that control is his, does the story stop? If so, he is your *main character*, and the story is about his quest to *gain* self-control.

So here we have a relatively simple scenario involving three principal characters only one of whom will serve as the *main character* in the story. Each character will possess a *treasure* that motivates her or his actions in the story, but only one will lay claim to the *treasure* that defines the story parameters and progress. For the other two characters, the magical granting of the *treasure* might remove her or him from the story, but the story itself would go on in any case, simply because the *intent* that drives its motor is not satisfied.

# DETERMINING THE TYPE OF INTENT

At its innermost core, the *grok approach* is based on the idea that the *main character* in any story possesses a single, overarching objective and that the objective can be formulated in terms of one of three possible *types of intent*. Specifically, she can *intend* to either:

- *gain* a *treasure* that she has never possessed,
- *regain* a *treasure* that she previously possessed, or
- *keep* a *treasure* that she currently possesses.

To fully employ the approach, therefore, the writer must know how to examine the *main character* to determine her *type of intent*.

In some cases, the determination is straightforward. The commander of an army brigade *attempting* to take a hill is a *gain* character who *intends* to *gain* control over battlefield real estate. A woman returning to her home town to restore her family honor is a *regain* character who *intends* to *regain* the good reputation that her family once enjoyed. The soldier in charge of defending an outpost is a *keep* character who *intends* to *keep* the outpost from being overrun. In other cases, it is not so cut-and-dried. The psychotic vigilante who prowls his neighborhood, armed to the teeth, might be trying to *keep* the neighborhood safe or to *regain* its former crime-free state—or even to *gain* revenge for a personal attack.

Regardless of whether the *type of intent* is easy to spot, however, it must be found and identified in the story creation process, so that its role in the development of the story can be used to maximum effect. Fortunately, like the identity of the *main character*, it may be determined by means of a simple thought experiment.

## THE TYPE-OF-INTENT THOUGHT EXPERIMENT

Just as the *main character* can be identified by granting a *treasure* that stops the story, so her *type of intent* can be identified by determining her response to the granting. Specifically, it can be found by means of another thought experiment, which may be stated as follows.

> To determine the *type of intent* of the *main character*, grant her (by magic) the *treasure* that stops the story and ascertain how she feels when the granting is done.

The generic answer, "good," might be accurate in its vagueness, but the vagueness itself renders it useless. To be of use in determining the *type of intent*, the result of this experiment must be stated using one of three terms—*enriched*, *restored*, or *relieved*. Specifically:

· A *main character* who feels *enriched* is a *gain* character.

· A *main character* who feels *restored* is a *regain* character.

· A *main character* who feels *relieved* is a *keep* character.

The general who is granted control of the hill feels *enriched*, because he possesses control of the sought-after battlefield real estate. The woman who is granted the good name of her family feels *restored*, because the family name resumes a place of honor that had been lost. The soldier whose outpost is safe feels *relieved*, because the threat to the outpost disappears.

When conducting this experiment, it is essential to think of the *treasure* as having been granted by magic rather than earned through the efforts of the *main character*. If it were earned, the feelings of the *main character* would likely always include a sense of relief that the fight for its attainment is over—thereby muddling the experiment. Only by granting the *treasure* through unearned grace can the writer derive the true *type of intent* by means of this experiment.

It is also important to keep in mind that the magical granting cannot take place before the *intent* and *treasure* are established. The general must already *intend* to *gain* control of the battlefield hill. The woman must already *intend* to *regain* the good name of her family. The outpost must already be threatened with attack, and the soldier must *intend* to *keep* it safe. Otherwise, the *type of intent* cannot exist.

## THE IMPORTANCE OF FEELINGS

It should come as no surprise that the *type-of-intent* thought experiment is based on how the *main character* feels rather than on what she thinks or plans or does. After all, feelings lie at the heart of all major human action, and with respect to our evolution as a species, they predate rational thought by millions of years.

Feeling-less actions occur every day in every corner of the world, but to serve significant roles in storytelling, actions must be motivated. And feelings are far more powerful than thoughts and rationales when it comes to motivating actions. They imbue the actions with purpose, meaning, and personal stakes, and they ensnare the audience in the world of the story through identification with its characters—especially the *main character*. They prompt characters to take certain steps and avoid taking others. They move the story forward and backward and jostle it side to side and up and down. Most important, however, they generate *intent*, which in turn gives rise to plans and actions.

In other words, plans and actions derive from feelings—which is why plot springs from character, not the other way around.

## EXAMINING THE TREASURE

As should be clear by now, the *treasure* is of paramount importance to the *grok approach*. Not only does it help identify the *main character*, it serves as part of the standard by which the audience measures progress in the story, and it participates in defining the story *theme*. To fully comprehend its significance and use, however, it is necessary to probe the gem-filled depths of its most fundamental aspects, a few of which include:

- Specificity
- Immediacy
- Genesis
- Time frame of concern
- Subjectivity
- Opposition
- Domain
- Authenticity

So strap on your pith helmet, grab your rock hammer and flashlight... and follow me.

## SPECIFICITY

Because the story depends so completely on the *main character* for its thrust and direction, the *treasure* is always defined in terms of her specific personal *goals* even if she is operating on behalf of someone else. For stories in which the *main character* pursues a *goal* on behalf of others instead of (or in addition to) herself, the *treasure* may be of value to those on whose behalf she is operating, but the value they impart to it is simply an enhancement to her own. Because the story rides on her back alone, it is her specific *treasure* that we-the-audience use to gauge progress in the story and judge its *theme*.

## IMMEDIACY

The value of the *treasure* must always be firmly rooted in the immediacy of the story at hand, not on any other episode in the life of the *main character*. As an example of such immediacy, consider a story in which the *main character* prepares to run a race in an *attempt* to be crowned its winner. In this case, her *intent* constitutes a *gain* action, and the *treasure* is victory in the race.

If the race is one that she has never run before or an annual event that she has run before and lost, it is easy to say that her *treasure* is one that she has never possessed. But what if she was victorious in one of its previous runnings? Is the *treasure* still one that she has never possessed? Absolutely. Why? Because until this year's race is run, its winner cannot be crowned, and neither she nor anyone else can claim possession of its victory. In this sense, her prior victories are irrelevant, because the story is about this year's race, not races that have been run in the past.

## GENESIS

*Treasures* do not spring to life out of thin air. Like the *intents* with which they are associated, they form at the potent intersections of desire and opportunity. As I noted in Chapter 5, the first structural act of any story can be aptly defined as "the tale of how the *main character* comes to obtain her *intent*." And since every *intent* involves a *treasure*, this definition necessarily involves the process by which we-the-audience discover the identity of the *treasure*.

In some cases, the *treasure* does not exist at the start of the story, and Act I reveals how it comes to be created. For example, the police detective has no criminal to pursue until the crime has been committed. Likewise, the miserly businessman has no world view to defend until the Christmas ghosts appear and threaten its existence. He may already possess the world view, but its preservation does not become a bona fide *treasure* until it is under attack.

In other cases, the *treasure* already exists when the story starts, and Act I consists of its piecewise revelation to the audience—for example, in the case of a woman who is already running for her life when the story opens. In such cases, we-the-audience must pick up clues along the way in Act I, so that we can understand the nature of her flight.

At the discretion of the writer, therefore, we-the-audience are either launched into the thick of a journey already in progress or are invited to watch the *treasure* being born. In either case, the revelation of the *treasure* exactly coincides with the creation of *intent*.

## TIME FRAME OF CONCERN

As I also noted in Chapter 5, every story is associated with a time frame of concern—that is, a general era that serves as the main focus for the *intent* of its *main character*. And the time frame of concern is directly related to the *type of intent* as follows.

- A *gain* character is focused on the future.
- A *regain* character is focused on the past.
- A *keep* character is focused on the present.

Because the *treasure* is the target of the *intent*, its time frame of concern behaves in exactly this same manner. And the behavior affects both the prerequisites for its existence and the manner in which it is revealed.

## Gain Stories

In a *gain* story, the *treasure* concerns an item or state of being that the *main character* has never before possessed—for example, a precious jewel or inner peace. Consequently, the time frame of concern for a *gain* story is the future in which the *treasure* might be possessed.

When creating a *gain* story, it is important to keep in mind that the prerequisites for its *treasure* might or might not exist at the beginning of the story. For example, a mountain climber who *intends* to become the first person to reach the summit of a dangerous peak is a *gain* character whose *treasure* consists of stepping onto the peak. In this case, the main prerequisite for the *treasure* (the existence of the peak) has existed as long as the peak has graced the landscape. The *treasure* itself does not exist, however, until the mountain climber acquires the *intent* to *gain* it. By contrast, the *treasure* for a police detective who seeks the identity of a murderer cannot exist until the murder is committed; therefore, its prerequisites do not exist until the victim falls dead. Yes, other murders have been committed in human history, and the detective might have solved other cases. But the story at hand involves only the murder that sets it in motion; consequently, its *treasure* cannot exist until someone is no longer breathing.

## Regain Stories

In a *regain* story, the *main character* possessed the *treasure* at one time but then lost it (or had it taken away or destroyed). Consequently, although the action takes place in the story-defined present, the storytelling may frequently refer to the past. To understand the importance of the *treasure*, for example, we-the-audience must be informed of its value through exposition, flashbacks, or out-of-the-gate summaries that establish the story world as it existed before possession of the *treasure* was lost.

The first act of *Back to the Future*, for example, places us squarely in the world to which the *main character*, Marty, belongs in 1985. By doing so, it shows us the world to which he strives to return when he finds himself displaced in time. Similarly, in *The Lord of the Rings: Fellowship of the Ring*, we are treated at the outset to a brief history of Middle Earth and how it came to acquire the state in which we find it when the story begins. We are introduced to the important characters and historical elements that lead up to the need for the *main character*, Frodo Baggins, to return the One Ring to the fires of Mount Doom, where it can be destroyed, thereby restoring (*regaining*) the land to its Sauron-free condition.

## Keep Stories

In a *keep* story, the *main character* possesses the *treasure* in the immediate time frame of the story; consequently, the story itself is focused mainly on the present, not the past or future. When a *keep* story references the past, it typically does so for one of four reasons—to:

· illustrate the nature and scope of the threat to the *treasure*,

· provide clues regarding how the *treasure* can be *kept*,

· describe obstacles that must be overcome to *keep* the *treasure*, or

· aid the opposing force in threatening the *treasure*.

In *A Christmas Carol*, for example, the Ghost of Christmas Past transports Scrooge into his own past and treats him to visions of his personal history—his lonely youth at a boarding school; his young sister, Fan, and her odd, obscure reference to their father being "so much kinder than he used to be"; his generous employer, Fezziwig; and the sad young fiancée who releases him from a marriage proposal because she has seen his "nobler aspirations fall off one by one." But none of these visions are meant to illustrate a world to which Scrooge aspires to be restored, as they would be in a *regain* story. They are, rather, nuclear-tipped cruise missiles fired by the Ghost of Christmas Past directly at the fortress of uncompassionate solitude that Scrooge has constructed around himself and *intends* to *keep*.

Likewise, in *Casablanca*, the melancholic scenes of Rick and Ilsa in Paris are not meant to illustrate the life that Rick aspires to *regain*. Instead, they show us-the-audience the circumstances that led to his retreat from the world. And to the extent that they represent Rick's own memories, they also serve as self-generated salvos against the walls of his fortress. Unlike Scrooge, however, Rick's internal fortress is not under direct assault from an outside entity. In *Casablanca*, Rick is attacked by the part of his own nature that has never completely put away the hurt and embraced the life of emotional solitude that he has constructed.

## SUBJECTIVITY

Because all *treasures* are specific to their *main characters*, each is subjective and is defined strictly in terms of the *main character* by whom it is possessed. Certain types of *treasures* may appear commonly in stories, but no *treasure* possesses inherent worth and meaning apart from its *main character*.

Such subjectivity does not imply that each *treasure* is important only to its *main character* in only a manner that cannot be understood by anyone else. On the contrary, to elicit sympathy in the audience, the *treasure* must possess tangible universality with regard to human experience. The subjectivity characteristic implies merely that the *treasure* derives its importance strictly from the *main character* and must, therefore, be entirely specific to her world, person, and *intent*.

A young man might cross a continent to recover a jar containing the ashes of his recently deceased father, whom he desires to see honored with a proper burial. Do the ashes possess objective value that would allow them to be traded in the marketplace? Probably not. But do they possess subjective worth to the *main character*? And does that subjective worth exhibit a universality that elicits sympathy with his quest? The answer is "yes" on both counts. Why? Because they are not merely ashes; they are the remains of a beloved parent—and most of us can understand the desire to honor the memory of a parent whom we loved.

When it comes to *treasures*, nothing is intrinsically worthwhile or worthless, and anything at all may serve as a *treasure* as long as it is significant to the *main character*. Recognition of this fact helps the writer avoid the tempting trap of seeking out conventional *treasures* for his *main character*. And by doing so, it frees him to find the deeper *treasure* that truly motivates his *main character*.

Money, for example, may appear at first glance to represent an objective *treasure* when, in fact, it is merely one means of achieving a greater objective. The street kid who steals money to put food on the table for his family is *intent* on *keeping* his family alive, and the money he steals is merely a means to do so. We-the-audience follow the story to see if he is able to *keep* his *treasure* (the well-being of his family) not to maintain a ledger of his thefts. And we judge the story progress, *outcome*, and *theme* by that measure alone. If he can attain his *treasure* without the use of money, so be it. Frankly, the money itself is not that intriguing.

Likewise, the aging con man who *intends* to steal a large sum of money from an unsuspecting mark might have any of a number of reasons for doing so—for example, to prove that he has not lost his touch. Yet in all but the most trivial scenarios, his motivation for pursuing the con transcends the mere getting of money. So the money, again, is merely a means of addressing some deeper *treasure*—and the deeper *treasure* is where the story lives. Why and to whom, for example, must he prove that he still has "the touch"? Is his virility or relevance in question? And if so, is the question being raised by a young lover whose attentions he suspects are drifting elsewhere? These are the types of questions that beg to be answered if the story is to possess depth. And it is difficult to explore them unless the writer discards the notion that the money itself possesses objective worth as a *treasure*.

Power and love are similar in this regard, because, like money, they possess no inherent worth. The significance of either depends strictly on the *main character* and her *intent*. They differ from money largely in that they take on a multitude of forms.

Take a story "about power," for example. Does it involve a king whose control over his subjects is threatened by a troublemaking freedom fighter? Or does it involve a middle-aged mother whose influence over her only son is threatened by the son's new girlfriend? Each of these scenarios possesses some form of power as its *treasure*, but only the first skirts the border of Conventional Powerland. The other explores the meaning of power in day-to-day family life. Its message is not trumpeted by a carnival barker screaming, "Hurry, hurry, hurry! Step this way to see a story about power!" It is conveyed by a savvy, back-alley insider whispering, "Pssssst! You want to see the truth about power? Follow me."

The same goes for love. Which kind does the story involve? Erotic? Familial? Obsessive? False? Delusional? And what is its object? A treasured pet? A boy at school? An idea or institution? And what is its underlying motivation? An insecurity that begs to be healed? The finding of a soul mate? The desire to help a hurting child?

Only by abandoning the notion that money, power, and love are objective *treasures* can the writer begin to explore the depths of his story. Meaningful *treasures* are not found on the well-lit superhighways of generic convention. They are found on the side roads of subjectivity—the gravelly, unmarked paths that lead away from the highway, across the desert, over the mountain pass, and into the wildly overgrown forest where lives the heart and soul of the *main character*.

## OPPOSITION

When developing a story, it is tempting to think conventionally of the *main character* as a "protagonist" who is directly opposed by an "antagonist" in her *attempt* to reach a story *goal*. By restating the *goal* of the *main character* in terms of her *intent* to pursue a *treasure*, however, the *grok approach* reveals the fundamental weakness in this conventional line of thinking. Specifically, it allows the writer to recognize the important difference between "antagonist" and "opposing character."

As I noted in Chapter 2, the *main character* is not always opposed by another character in the story. Sometimes she is opposed by Nature itself. But even in stories that involve opposition by other characters, the opposition might not be specifically directed at preventing the *main character* from achieving her *treasure*. It might simply result as a natural consequence of the other character's pursuit of a personal *goal*.

In the film *Whale Rider*, for example, Paikea's grandfather, Koro, does not focus all of his energies on directly opposing her *attempt* to *gain* what she feels to be her proper place in the tribe. He may do so incidentally when her actions interfere with his own efforts to *regain* the cultural vigor of the tribe, but his main energies are directed at restoring that vigor, not on opposing Paikea in her quest. Likewise, in *Back to the Future*, none of the characters in the world of 1955 directly tries to prevent Marty from *regaining* his place in the world of 1985. In fact, the only character who is aware of his displacement, Doc Brown, tries to help Marty *succeed* in achieving his *goal*. The other characters may complicate Marty's efforts to pursue his *intent*, but none sees opposing those efforts as his or her *goal*; therefore, none can be rightly labeled as his "antagonist."

The writer who thinks merely in terms of using an antagonist to explicitly oppose the *intent* of the *main character* does himself and his story a disservice. In most cases, such conventional thinking cripples the ability of the story to push down roots and become the strong and vibrant organic entity that it could be, engaging its audience on multiple levels and probing the depths of the *issues* at its core.

## DOMAIN

Every *treasure* may be said to exist in one of two domains, depending on whether or not it is observable directly by the audience. The domains and their definitions are as follows.

- *External*—The *treasure* exists outside the *main character* and can be observed by any spectator in the story world.
- *Internal*—The *treasure* exists within the *main character* and cannot be observed except by inference.

In other words, we-the-audience could stand on a hill with a pair of binoculars, gazing into the story world and observe directly whether an *external treasure* has been *gained, regained,* or *kept*. But we would need to climb inside the *main character* to determine the status of an *internal treasure*. And if we are not allowed to do so—for example, when the story is conveyed through performance on a stage or screen or in a novel that does not employ an omniscient point of view—then the *internal treasure* must manifest in some outward form from which it can be inferred.

By way of analogy, it is easy to observe the rising and setting of the sun and to conclude that either the sun is orbiting Earth or vice versa. (It turns out to be the latter.) But it is quite difficult to observe a planet orbiting a distant star—which is why the question of whether other stars have planets has only recently (in 1992) begun to be answered (in the affirmative). How do astronomers determine whether a distant star is orbited by planets? By looking for behaviors that might be caused by the planets. That is to say, by inference.

The same principle applies to the expression of *internal treasures* in a story. We-the-audience require tangible evidence regarding the nature of the *internal treasure* and whether or not it is ultimately *gained, regained,* or *kept*. And since we cannot observe the *treasure* itself, we must be shown the effects of its attainment and allowed to deduce its existence on our own. Fortunately, we tend to be very good at reading between the lines and interpreting the motivations that lie behind the behaviors of our fellow human beings. In most cases, we do not even need to be taught how to do so; we evolved the talent as a matter of survival.

In *Back to the Future*, for example, Marty finds himself in a predicament that is very easy to observe from outside the story world. He has been displaced from his home and *intends* to return. Consequently, his *treasure* is *external* and his *success* or *failure* to attain it is easily shown. In *Casablanca*, on the other hand, Rick possesses an *internal treasure*—that is, the emotional fortress that he has built around himself. And because it is not observable directly, its existence must be conveyed through his behaviors. And it is the changes in those behaviors (or lack thereof) that reveal his *success* or *failure* in the end.

## AUTHENTICITY

When examining any *treasure* it is important to carefully determine its authenticity—that is, whether it represents a genuine *treasure* or merely a *trophy*. Such *trophies* serve as stand-ins for their actual *treasures* and, in this sense, each constitutes a mirage—a shimmering illusion on the desert plain that masks the true obelisk behind it.

The expensive car that the ambitious young man pursues as a symbol of success is merely a *trophy*; his true *intent* is to *gain* a feeling of success. The same can be said of the diploma that the woman of humble means *attempts* to acquire as proof that she can rise above her background—when, in fact, she seeks only the feeling that she has done so. Or the companionship of the young lover that the older woman *attempts* to *keep* in order to retain the feeling that she is still vital—when her true *goal* is to *keep* the feeling regardless of whether or not the lover is in the picture.

In each case, the *trophy* may be thought of as the *outer* manifestation of an *inner* feeling—for example, the feeling of having achieved success, the feeling of having risen above one's background, and the feeling of being vital. And it is from the examination of such *outer* and *inner goals* and the related distinctions between *trophies* and *truth* that many story-elevating nuances may be brought to light.

## Outer and Inner Goals

"Well," one might say, "there is nothing so mirage-like in all this. It is quite common for people to seek out tangible measures of the states of things, especially when they want those states to change. We call such measures *goals*." To which the *grok*-ist says, "Precisely." The purpose of this categorization is not to negate the value of *goals*—it is to take a scalpel to them, peel back the slimy membranes inside, and reveal that every such *goal* is constructed of two different organs, *outer* and *inner*. The *outer goal* is the *trophy*—the tangible, demonstrable, hey-look-what-I-did measure of whether or not the *inner goal* has been achieved. The *inner goal* is the feeling that the character anticipates experiencing upon achieving the *outer goal*. And only when the story has been wheeled out of the operating room, its two *goals* having been successfully separated, can the next question be asked: Which one drives the story?

Here's a hint: It's not the *outer goal*.

Characters in stories are fundamentally motivated not by their *outer goals* but by the *inner* feelings that they either hope to enjoy when they *succeed* in their pursuits or fear undergoing if they *fail*. So in this sense, the *trophy* masks the true motivation of a character, which actually lies in the realm of her feelings. To understand the true motivations of the character, therefore, the writer must look past the *outer goal* and examine the *inner goal*—that is, the feeling that the character is *attempting* to experience or avoid by pursuing her *intent*.

Not only is the concept of *outer* and *inner goals* important to the development of any story, it is critical to its reception by the audience. Why? Because we-the-audience receive any story through two simultaneous channels—our heads and our hearts. Our heads look to the *outer* elements of the story; our hearts look to its *inner* elements—specifically, the feelings that lie at the core of the character motivations. When it comes to measuring story progress, our heads take the lead and look for *outer* clues of movement. But when it comes to judging the story with respect to its *theme*, our hearts step in and grab the controls. In fact, the *intent* of any character in a story can itself be divided into two distinct parts—the *what* (*outer goal*) and the *why* (*inner goal*).

In *Whale Rider*, sanction by the tribal authority figure is the *what*; the anticipated *feeling* of having attained one's proper place is the *why*. In *Back to the Future*, the return to the world of 1985 is the *what*; the fear of *feeling* forever trapped in a world to which one does not belong is the *why*. In *Casablanca*, the successful defense of an emotional fortress is the *what*; the fear of having to deal once again with hurts that one has locked away is the *why*.

The *what* and the *why* of *intent*. Remember them for Part Two. They both play vital roles in expressing the story *theme*.

## Trophies and Truth

To refer to the *trophy* as a "mirage," as I did above, is not to ascribe to it a negative connotation. Illusion can be used for good or evil. The Buddhist monk who uses mental sleight of hand to stretch the minds of his students can be thought of as an illusionist. So can the apothecary who flavors a child's medicine to taste like candy. In both of these cases, the illusion is meant to do good, not evil.

Some *trophies* can be *false* or misleading to be sure, but even such *trophies* can prove useful for developing a story, especially if a character mistakenly seeks an *outer goal* in pursuit of an *inner goal* of which she is not aware. A young woman might pursue an election victory, for example, when what she really desires is the emotional acceptance of her politically powerful father. If the writer grants her the victory but not the acceptance, and the story does not stop, he must probe the story further to determine her actual *treasure*. And by so doing, he will find out what is really driving the story.

Because of its tangible (*outer*) nature, a *trophy* can be thought of as the concrete answer to the question that we-the-audience are compelled to ask regarding the *main character* and her *treasure* and *intent*—that is: How will we know if she *succeeds* or *fails*? Should we look for the fighter to stay on his feet until the bell rings to end Round 15? Should we hope for the expulsion of the alien creature from the shuttle craft? Or the exposure of the killer at an awards dinner?

How will we know?

# EXAMPLE STORY ANALYSES

To understand how the *grok approach* applies to story development, it is instructive to analyze existing stories in light of its elements and theory. The stories analyzed below were not developed by means of the *grok approach*, but their success as well-told stories provides clues and insights regarding the approach and its applications. And yes, I could have chosen any number of other stories or selected stories from other story forms, but I did not. The titles of those I did choose (and the *types of intent* of their *main characters*) are:

+ *Whale Rider* (*gain*)
+ *Back to the Future* (*regain*)
+ *Casablanca* (*keep*)

If you have not yet seen these films, you really must.

## WHALE RIDER (GAIN)

In *Whale Rider*, the *main character*, Paikea, is a young girl who feels compelled to attain her proper place in the society of the Maori tribe into which she has been born. She is not a power-hungry vixen using her wiles to attain a position of status for the satisfaction or perks that come with doing so. She is a girl who cares very much for her tribe and feels compelled to become involved in its health and history.

Paikea does not *attempt* to *regain* a position that she once possessed and then lost. Neither does she *attempt* to *keep* a position that is under threat of being lost. Rather, she *attempts* to *gain* a position that she has never before possessed. Consequently, Paikea is a *gain* character, and her *treasure* is her proper place among her people. This *treasure* is entirely subjective and is not one that her peers deem to be of objective worth and seek for their own. Her underlying desire to find her proper place in the world renders the *treasure* universal, however, because the desire is common to human experience.

The problem for Paikea is that the position she desires is one of leadership—specifically, the type that is traditionally reserved for males. And the problem is compounded by the fact that her grandfather, Koro, is a strict traditionalist *intent* on *regaining* the cultural health of the tribe but only in the context of its traditions, including male-only leadership. When Paikea tries to take part in his efforts to groom a new leader, he prevents her from doing so—angrily and in no uncertain terms. And when she acquires (by way of an ally) a fighting skill that he believes should be reserved for males only, he accuses her of dishonoring the tribe.

It is Koro's elevated position in the tribe and family that allows him to exercise power over Paikea—the power that she must struggle against as she pursues satisfaction of her *intent*. And it is her strong and unrequited love for him that prevents her from abandoning her quest or *attempting* to achieve her *goals* in selfish and disrespectful ways. But her primary quest, to *gain* her proper place in the tribe, has nothing directly to do with power or love.

In this case, we have a strong *main character* with a clear *intent* whose efforts are hindered by a character whose *intent* is also clear. The hindering character (Koro) is not an antagonist who expends energy directly opposing Paikea. He does oppose her actions when they interfere with his own efforts to *regain* the cultural health of the tribe, but the focus of his attention is on restoring that health, not on opposing Paikea.

These are not two characters on opposite sides of a clearly drawn line in the sand; they are characters on the same side of the line but with very different ideas about what to do there. Consequently, they are sympathetic characters whose *intents* concern a common, overarching goal (the cultural health of the tribe) but who possess opposing views about how to achieve it. That makes for very powerful storytelling.

By the end of the story, Paikea *succeeds* in *gaining* her *treasure*, and we-the-audience are *pleased* that she does so—not only for its satisfying conclusion to her personal journey but because of the positive effect that her *success* has on the cultural health of her people. Even Koro is left happy, having *failed* in his own *attempt* to *regain* the health of the tribe on his terms but pleased to see the health restored nonetheless.

## BACK TO THE FUTURE (REGAIN)

In *Back to the Future*, high-school student Marty McFly befriends a slightly mad scientist, Doc Brown, and is accidentally thrust 30 years into the past by means of the scientist's time machine. When Marty finds himself displaced into the world of his home town, circa 1955, he sets his sights on returning to his own place and time.

Marty's journey in the film is one of *attempting* to return to the world he knows. Consequently, he is a *regain* character whose primary *goal* is to *regain* his proper place in time. His place in the world of 1985 is the *treasure* that existed (for him) at one time but was lost. That *treasure* does not exist at the outset of the story and cannot exist, in fact, until the cascading circumstances of Act I dislodge him from that world and propel him three decades into the past. In this case, Marty becomes aware of his *treasure* at the same time we-the-audience do—that is, upon its creation.

As a *regain* character, Marty's *timeframe of concern* is located squarely in his personal past (the actual future). And his *treasure* is subjective and specific—in fact, only one other character knows that it exists. It is also universal, born from the simple desire to return home.

Part of the strength of *Back to the Future* lies in the fact that much of Marty's effort demonstrates a single *type of intent*—that of *regaining*. While *attempting* to *regain* his proper place in time, for example, he must also *attempt* to *regain* the potential for union between the boy and girl who are to become his parents. As with any other well-told story, the film is filled with scenes involving all three *types of intent*—for example, when he seeks out and enlists the aid of the 30-years-younger Doc Brown (thereby *gaining* an ally) and when he uses his skateboarding skills to avoid capture (*keeping* himself safe from harm) by Biff, the bully who serves as his primary opposing character in 1955. But his primary *intent* is to *regain* his place in the world as he knows it, and that is the *type of intent* that informs most of the story.

Power and love affect the story, but not as its primary movers. Marty's affection for Doc Brown compels him to try to prevent a tragic fate that he knows awaits him in the future. And the teenage crush that his future mother develops on him when he first shows up in 1955 greatly complicates his journey. But notwithstanding the theme song by Huey Lewis and the News, *Back to the Future* is not about power or love. It is about a boy *attempting* to return home.

By the end of the story, Marty *succeeds* in *regaining* his *treasure*, and we-the-audience are happy that he does so. The fact that he ends up improving the world to which he returns to is a happy *consequence* of his journey, but it is not his *intent* at any point. So here, too, is a story in which the *main character succeeds* in pursuing his *intent*, and we-the-audience are left feeling *pleased* that he does so.

## CASABLANCA (KEEP)

In *Casablanca*, the *main character*, Rick, is a *keep* character whose *treasure* is the emotional fortress that he has built around himself. When the threat to that *treasure* appears in the form of his former lover, Ilsa, he *intends* to defend the fortress and *keep* it intact. His *treasure* is very personal and subjective, and it is entirely *internal*—observable only by inference from his behaviors. Because it stems from unresolved pain, however, it is also universal.

When the story opens, Rick has removed himself physically and psychologically from the war-torn world of 1941 Europe and has developed what appears to be an impenetrable emotional fortress, the walls of which take the form of active neutrality and a stubborn resistance to taking sides. And when the story starts, nothing in his world threatens the security of that fortress. Then Ilsa walks into his nightclub, and all hell breaks loose. She is the meteor zooming in from the heavens to smash the walls of his world. Soon Rick finds himself torn apart, then caring again and becoming less neutral. When the Czech freedom fighter Victor Lazlo orders the nightclub band leader to play *La Marseillaise* to drown a spontaneous Nazi chorus of *Die Wacht am Rhein*, the band leader looks to Rick for permission to do so—and Rick grants it. And when a young bride is faced with the prospect of rendering sexual favors to Captain Renault to obtain safe passage for herself and her trusting husband, Rick ensures that her husband wins enough money at the roulette table to pay for the passage without having to give up the favors, upsetting Renault in the process.

None of the characters directly oppose Rick's *intent* to *keep* his *treasure*; therefore, none can be rightly labeled as an "antagonist." Other characters do entreat him to let down his guard, and each plays a part in assaulting the fortress itself—for example, by seductive enticement (Ilsa) or grating challenge (Nazi Major Strasser)—but none of them sets herself or himself directly in opposition to his *intent*.

And although money, power, and love all constitute factors in the story, none is directly related to the story *goal*. The petty crook Ugarte plans to sell the letters of transit he obtained from the murdered German couriers, and certainly, the love that Rick still feels for Ilsa—as well as her love for Victor—entwine and complicate the story lines. But the driving force in the story is internal to Rick and centers on whether or not he will let down his guard, for his own sake and that of those around him. It is not directly related to money, power, or love.

Rick is a *keep* character whose *treasure* is the emotional fortress that he has built around himself, and the story is not over until the threat to his *treasure* either disappears on its own, is vanquished completely, or wins out. By the end of the story, he *fails* to *keep* his *treasure*—in spectacular, noble, romantic fashion—and we are *pleased* that he does so. So in this case, the *main character fails* in his *attempt* to *keep* a *treasure*, and we-the-audience are *pleased* for his *failure*.

Very interesting.

Let's keep it in mind for Part Two.

# Chapter 7

## THE SHORT TOUR

The college from which I received my engineering degrees is located outside of Denver, Colorado in a small town that also serves as home to a well-known brewery (think *Smokey and the Bandit*). When I was an undergraduate student, the brewery offered two types of tours—a "long tour" and a "short tour."

The long tour led patrons on an information-packed journey through the brewery, highlighting its illustrious history, the temperature-controlled rooms where the barley is carefully malted, the vast array of copper kettles where the beer is fermented, and the bustling packaging lines where the beer is bottled or canned, boxed, and sent on its way across America.

The short tour made a beeline from the lobby to the bar.

Welcome to the short tour.

Plot derives from character, not the other way around. In every well-told story, the action revolves around a *core ensemble* of central characters who perform the primary functional roles that advance the story and give it emotional heft. Of all the characters in the *core ensemble*, one is more important than the others and occupies the special role of *main character*.

The *main character* performs four major tasks in the telling of the story. Specifically, she:

- serves as a vehicle through which the audience member can ride along and experience the world of the story;
- generates the story events by means of her *intents* and actions;
- provides the audience with an indicator of story progress; and
- expresses the *theme* of the story by means of her decisions, actions, and ultimate *success* or *failure*.

The motivations of the *main character* are best described not in terms of what she *wants*, but in terms of what she *intends*. *Wants* are static and do not require action. *Intents* demand action and prompt the *main character* to pursue the satisfaction of the *wants*.

The overall journey of the *main character* in any story is best described in terms of a *type of intent* and *treasure*. The *type of intent* of the *main character* can be expressed in one of three ways—to:

· *gain* a *treasure* that she has never possessed,

· *regain* a *treasure* that she previously possessed, or

· *keep* a *treasure* that she currently possesses.

The *type of intent* determines the direction of the story and the means by which the audience will gauge its progress. It also clarifies the underlying motivations of the *main character*, establishes the plausibility of events, promotes consistency in character actions, reveals the story time frame of concern, and helps define points of structural reference.

The writer can identify the *main character* by performing a simple thought experiment to find the *treasure* the magical granting of which will stop the story in its tracks. And the thought experiment can also be extended to determine the *type of intent* for the *main character* by assessing her *feelings* upon magical receipt of the *treasure*. Specifically:

· If she feels *enriched*, she is a *gain* character.

· If she feels *restored*, she is a *regain* character.

· If she feels *relieved*, she is a *keep* character.

All *treasures* are subjective and each is defined strictly according to the *main character* with whom it is associated. The significance ascribed to any *treasure* might align with a sense of conventional worth but is not required to do so.

Some *treasures* are *external* and observable by any spectator of the story world; others are *internal* and can only be inferred from the behaviors of the *main characters* who possess them. Most *treasures* are associated with *outer goals* that arise from *inner goals*. The *outer goal* for any *main character* illustrates her tangible target; the *inner goal* represents the feeling that she anticipates possessing if she *succeeds* in her *attempt* to attain the *outer goal*— or fears possessing if she *fails*. We-the-audience look to the *outer goals* to gauge story progress. We use the *inner goals* to judge the story with respect to its meaning and *theme*.

And that is the gist of the *grok approach* summed up in one very big nutshell. So go take a break with your beverage of choice and let it all sink in. And when you return, we'll take up this matter of *theme*.

# Part Two

## Thematic Imprinting

# Chapter 8

## THE GHOST IN THE MACHINE

Great stories invite their audiences to participate in the storytelling experience, not merely as onlookers but as fully empathetic visitors to their imagined worlds. The best of those worlds are populated with characters whose plights and journeys are easily identified with and whose circumstances arise naturally from disturbances in the day-to-day operations of the worlds themselves.

The trick for the writer is to create such worlds while disguising the fact that she has done so—to make it appear as if she is merely documenting events to which she happens to be privy, regardless of how inconceivable it might be that she could actually have obtained the knowledge that she is able to relate in the story. It is the ability to master this faculty of illusion and to thereby create stories that are simultaneously surprising, insightful, and self-consistent that makes a writer great.

The principles of the *grok approach* outlined in Part One of this book are designed to help the writer create stories that manifest clear, consistent actions and *intents* on the part of her characters. And because plot springs from character, such clarity and consistency serves to align the invisible spine of the story and helps lead to the creation of stories that are organic, engaging, and satisfying on many levels.

But deep inside any great story lies an unseen engine that generates its movements, including those of the *main character* whose *intent* drives its actions and events. This great invisible engine churns silently at the core of the story and transforms the fundamental entreaty of its creator from "Let me tell you about something that happened" into its far-more-potent counterpart, "Let me tell you something you need to know."

This engine has a name. Its name is *"theme."*

In an abstract sense, the *theme* of any story may be thought of as an entity in and of itself—a living statement hidden behind the mask that the story shows to its audience. It is, quite literally, the "ghost in the machine" that provides the machine with its soul.

# THEME AS ARTISTIC DECLARATION

At its most fundamental level, the *theme* of a story is an artistic declaration made by the writer. In this context, it may be reasonably equated to the artistic statement made by a painter in her art. As we-the-audience stand gazing at a painting on display in a gallery or museum, we are likely to be aware primarily of its outward manifestation. After all, in strictly reductionist terms, we are privy to nothing more than the paint applied to the canvas. But because we are human, our capacity for poetic faith can step in and blind us to the here-and-now reality of that paint—that it is a physical substance we could reach out and pick at with our fingers if we liked (and the guards were not looking). And that blinding frees us to forget about the paint and to focus on the painting instead—its patterns, forms, colors, and representations—and to thereby see it in a broader, richer context. If the painting is done well and is born from the honest *intent* of its creator to express some bit of her perspective, however small, regarding the world, our focus may shift yet again, so that we forget about the painting altogether and experience it subliminally—by which I mean become aware (but not necessarily conscious) of its *theme*.

In this way, a *thematic* message from the soul of the painter is stuffed into a metaphorical bottle, tossed into a metaphorical sea, and conveyed across space and time to the not-so-metaphorical soul of us-the-audience. It is this magical process of soul-to-soul messaging that sets great art apart from purely rational forms of communication.

When the process works in its most seamless form, we-the-audience are not aware of the *theme* as being conveyed to us in this fashion. We are aware only of having encountered and engaged with the painting at some inner level, and each of us merely absorbs the *theme* as a feeling. The feeling might comfort us, challenge us, or upset us, but the magic of its conveyance lies in the fact that it is subtle and silent, operating in a deep internal realm where rational language is mute and irrelevant.

This same sort of magic can manifest in any of the arts, of course, including architecture, where solid, unmoving structures can invoke feelings of grandeur, freedom, or intimacy or even convey whole philosophies through subtleties encoded in their designs. As Frank Lloyd Wright said of Unity Temple, the church he designed at the turn of the last century for his own Unitarian congregation in Oak Park, Illinois:

> "That was my first expression of this eternal idea, which is at the center and the core of all true modern architecture—a sense of space... No sense of containment, only a sense of interior space, protected from the exterior by features... You are still free when you're in here, and even more free than when you're out on the street."

And if you have ever had the pleasure of visiting Unity Temple and stepping from its low-ceilinged foyer into the sanctuary with its high, louvered art-glass ceiling, clerestory windows, and ranks of intimately situated pews, you have witnessed first-hand the expression of *theme* in a building that is inanimate only with respect to its physicality. In the experience of the visitor, it is vibrantly alive.

On the other side of the philosophical spectrum, the Fascist German and Italian architecture of the early 20th century was designed to intimidate and overwhelm the onlooker, thereby conveying the feeling, and reinforcing the state-sanctioned message, that the individual is subservient to the state. It is a *theme* encoded into the bricks and mortar of the Fascist buildings just as surely as the number of days in the calendar year is encoded in the structure of the Pyramid of Kukulkan at Chichén Itzá[*].

So yes, *theme* matters. And it manifests everywhere, especially in works of art and well-told stories.

## THE HOW-TO OF THEMATIC DECLARATION

Given the importance of *theme* to artistic expression, the fundamental question for the writer who wishes to imbue her story with a clear, unspoken declaration of *theme* is: How do I do that? And here again, the conventional approach to thinking about stories provides no help at all in finding an answer. Unlike the weary advice about *wanting*, however—that a strong character must *want* something—the matter of *theme* is tired-old-saw-less, devoid of any accepted clichés that synopsize the manner in which the question should be approached. Which leaves the writer grasping at shadows for an answer, without the slightest guarantee that the answer exists or the merest of clues regarding where it might be found.

At least with the old-saw question about *wanting*, the writer is given a question to ask that narrows the field of answers, if only slightly—that is: What does my character *want*? The question about *theme*, however, is even less well-posed, taking the bland, generic form: What is the *theme* of my story? But if the writer is savvy enough to ask the question in the first place, the question itself is pretty much useless in guiding the way to its answer.

The writer seeking the *theme* of her story can look to examples, of course—sifting through stories told through the ages and studying them to determine their *themes* in the hope of finding one that seems akin or suited to the story she is creating. Or she can try to put into words the feelings that have prompted her to create the story in the first place. But even if she is

---

[*] Each of the four sides of the pyramid includes a staircase consisting of 91 steps, which adds to a total of 364 steps for the pyramid as a whole. If you consider the platform at the top of the pyramid to be the uppermost step, the total number of steps equals 365, the approximate number of days in a calendar year.

able to find the *theme* in this way, nothing in the process of doing so explicitly links that *theme* to the storytelling itself. Consequently, its discovery might provide her with insight and a general notion of the impact of her story, but it is unable to reveal any direct connections between the *theme* and the storytelling—or to endow her with clues regarding how to fix or enhance its expression.

What is needed, really, to address this whole matter of *theme* in a story is what one might call a *"thematic grammar"*—that is, a complete manner of thinking about, developing, and expressing the *theme* of any story in a way that conveys that *theme* at a subliminal level and complies with a few simple rules. The rules of this *thematic grammar* would need to be easy to learn and apply, and they would need to be self-consistent, like those of mathematics, so that they would apply across the entire story universe, just as (we presume) the rules of addition and subtraction that are valid here on Earth are also valid on the other side of the galaxy.

And y'know what would really be great? If the rules and expressions of this *thematic grammar* correlated directly with the basic principles of a storytelling approach that focused on the *intent* of the *main character* as the driving force in any story—like, say, the *grok approach* presented in Part One.

Yessir, if someone would just create a *thematic grammar* that fit those criteria, the world of storytelling might benefit greatly and any writer who applied it to her stories might find herself blessed with the kinds of insight that lead to the creation of enduring stories that speak to all cultures and eras.

Well, here's a bit of good news.

Someone has.

# Chapter 9

## FOUNDATIONS OF THEMATIC GRAMMAR

Let me be clear about one thing at the outset. The purpose of *thematic grammar* is not to clutter your storytelling toolbox with yet another take on a weary old manner of thinking. Nor is it to turn the storytelling world upside down by introducing radical concepts that have no correlation to existing ideas. Its purpose is simply to take a fresh look at the slippery, amorphous goo that goes by the name of "story *theme*" and divide it into pieces that can be studied to reveal their foundations—then to construct from those foundations a straightforward means of thinking about and expressing the message that lies at the heart of any great story in its truest and clearest form.

In some ways, the search for a workable *thematic grammar* can be likened to the quest for scientific knowledge, which tends to advance over time in fits and starts. Ancient civilizations, for example, possessed a detailed understanding of the movements of the planets, but it was not until Copernicus[*] advanced the idea of a sun-centered solar system and Johannes Kepler followed up with laws that described planetary motion with reasonable accuracy that significant advances in astronomy could to be made. Likewise, the light of the sun has bathed the Earth for more than four billion years, but it was not until Isaac Newton used prisms to separate that light into its component wavelengths that humanity began to understand the qualities of light.

I do not pretend that *thematic grammar* is on a par with the movement of planets or the nature of light, but the analogy is apt, nonetheless. It is not unreasonable, in fact, to think of its use as a prismatic path toward the practical understanding of story *theme*.

## LAYING THE GROUNDWORK

Having thus defined the purpose of *thematic grammar*, we may begin to lay its groundwork. And we do so at its very point of origin, somewhere near the roots of storytelling itself... in the deep past of humankind.

---

[*] Actually, Copernicus was not the first to propose the idea of a sun-centered solar system. The idea had been put forth by Greek mathematician Aristarchus of Samos circa 200 B.C.E. but was rejected in favor of the Earth-centered theories of Aristotle and Ptolemy.

# EXAMINING THE ROOTS OF STORYTELLING

Unless and until our species solves the problem of time travel and sends a probe or explorer into our distant past, no one can claim with authority to know how or why the practice of storytelling began. Like intrepid investigators, however, we are free to analyze its petrified roots—at least those exposed by the winds of time—and to speculate regarding its evolution and the ongoing purpose of its remnants in modern-day life. Whether you chalk up the practice to learned-and-taught behavior or to the expression of a genetic imperative that helps our species to survive, the study is revealing.

The earliest forms of storytelling appear to have served, at least in part, as means of preserving the norms of the cultures that spawned them. The ancient Indian Panchatantra, for example, consists of morality tales that address five fundamental principles for the prudent conduct of life, such as those related to loss or discord among friends. The fables of Aesop, too, are meant to relate, and thereby preserve, principles of conduct deemed by the storyteller to foster the smooth operation of life and society. And even full-blown myths and historical tales, such as those found in the Epic of Gilgamesh, Greek mythology, and the Bible are not value-neutral reports of imagined events. They are, instead, stories invested with a grand purpose—to pass on and preserve accepted norms regarding the proper way to live.

So there is the first bit of insight to be gained by probing the ancient roots of storytelling—the notion that the practice did not spring up as a value-neutral form of amusement. That its heritage is one of subtle sermonizing, and its role as entertainment may well be a secondary trait.

If we examine this notion closely, we discover that it sets an important standard for both our study and the creation of *thematic grammar*, itself. Specifically, it dictates that our *thematic grammar* cannot be developed in a value-neutral context and that storytelling, at its core, involves the conveyance of value judgments, especially with regard to the conduct of life. The expression of such judgments may be explicit or implicit, heavy-handed or subtle to the point of near invisibility, but it is vital to the matter of *theme* in the telling of stories.

Value-less information, even if it is doled out as a sequence of events, does not constitute a story. Notwithstanding the storytelling advice commonly attributed to either Ernest Hemingway, Peter De Vries, or Frank Capra that, "If you're looking for messages, get Western Union," any story that aims to do more than transfer data must contain at its core a value judgment of some kind—even if the judgment consists of nothing more than the unspoken solicitation of approval or disapproval for the actions of its characters.* And although the inclusion of a value judgment does not

---

* In fact, value judgments are often used to set the stage for even our most mundane, day-to-day tales—for example, "My brother-in-law is an idiot..."

guarantee a great story, great stories do tend to include such judgments at their cores.

"Love conquers all." "Blood is thicker than water." "Self-importance leads to ruin." "Power corrupts." These are more than mere pronouncements; they are value judgments, and each has served at some point as the underlying message in a well-told story. The story might not have been created for the explicit purpose of conveying the message, but the message is encoded in the story nonetheless.

We may conclude, therefore, that any writer who aspires to create a story worthy of genuine merit must recognize that its core will contain a value judgment of some kind. The writer might or might not be conscious of the judgment, but the judgment will exist nonetheless, even if it springs completely from matters of personal importance of which the writer herself is unaware.

And it will manifest in the telling.

## BRINGING THE MESSAGE DOWN TO EARTH

To take the next step in our groundwork-laying process, we must pull the story-as-value-judgment idea down from the great stage of pronouncements writ large across the heavens and drag it into the dangerous and intimate realm of the trusted back-alley insider whispering in the shadows of our souls. And when we do so, the pronouncements undergo an important transformation in which they shed their grand and opulent shells, exposing the luminous pearls of truth underneath. And herein lies a wonderful secret; it is the radiant light of such pearls that elevates a story from good to great or great to magnificent—and the writer who shines that light onto her story does the story and its audience a valuable service.

The point of this imagery is simply to convey a fundamental idea of *thematic grammar*—that to understand the *theme* of any story, the writer must prevent herself from thinking of value judgments as grand proclamations trumpeted from the heavens and must think of them, instead, as pieces of advice passed between intimate friends... the kind of advice that might be offered over coffee at the end of a catch-up lunch. The writer is one friend; the individual audience member is the other. And the message is the piece of advice passed between them while waiting for the check.

When looked at in this way, the expression of value judgments in storytelling has less to do with bullhorn-worthy shouting than it does with pillow talk. And that metaphor refers not only to the subtlety or lack thereof with which the message is put forth; it refers to the essence of the message itself and its purpose for inhabiting the story. Bullhorn-worthy advice amounts to little more than a position statement and focuses attention on the writer and her ability to shout. Pillow-talk advice is aimed at the concerns of the receiver—which is why it serves as a potent means of conveying a message.

## PERSONALIZING THE MESSAGE

Having lassoed the writ-large message in the heavens and brought it safely to Earth, we must figure out how to adapt it to life on land. Or to put it less metaphorically, having established that messages in storytelling are akin to advice between friends, it behooves us to consider how such advice is typically given and to use the findings to inform our development of *thematic grammar*. And when we do so, it becomes evident immediately that all such advice can be expressed in one of two basic forms:

· You should...

· You should not...

For example:

· You should exercise more.

· You should not ignore the warning signs of cancer.

It is far less likely, for example, that one friend will say to another, "Nothing endures but change," than it is that she will offer, "You should forget about him and move on." "Nothing endures but change," is an aphorism that one might find painted on a faux-weathered wooden sign in a high-end tourist novelty shop. "You should forget about him and move on," is an offering between confidants—from one who cares to one in need of caring. And it includes not only the advice itself but the encouragement to take it.

By personalizing the message in this way, the advice-giving forms of "You should" and "You should not" strip the message of its aphoristic trappings and render it raw and essential—something that demands to be considered and either accepted or ignored. And by doing so, they sharpen the message and render it worthy as the basis for a *theme*.

## SURVEYING THE GROUNDWORK

As simple as they seem at first glance, the ideas outlined above are robust enough by themselves to form the groundwork of a true *thematic grammar*. To recap and summarize:

Deep at the core of storytelling practice churns the age-old impulse to pass on (and thereby preserve) a norm or value, especially one regarding the conduct of life. Consequently, great stories tend to contain at their centers a value judgment regarding how to live. The judgment springs from the feelings and opinions of the writer herself—even those of which she might not be aware. And it manifests to the audience as a subliminal message that comprises the heart of the story *theme*. Although such messages might lend themselves to shouting through a bullhorn, they are better thought of and approached as pillow-talk—advice whispered softly from the writer to each of her audience members (rather than to the audience as a whole). And the advice itself can be couched in one of two basic forms: "You should" or "You should not."

Groundwork successfully laid. Let's bring out the heavy equipment and build the structure.

# ELEMENTS OF THEMATIC GRAMMAR

Just as linguistic grammar consists of individual parts of speech and the rules by which they combine to form sentences, so *thematic grammar* consists of individual elements and the rules that govern their interactions to convey a story *theme*. Fortunately, the elements of *thematic grammar* are far fewer in number than those of linguistic grammar—even that of Esperanto[*]. In fact, there are only three, which are:

* *Proposition*

* *Outcome*

* *Reaction*

The *proposition* is a statement made by the story concerning how to live—what one might call the snapshot of its ghost. The *outcome* is the *succeed-*or-*fail* result of an *attempted endeavor* contained in the *proposition*. The *reaction* is the gut response elicited in the audience upon witnessing the *outcome* of the *attempt*.

When properly combined, these elements work together to imprint the *theme* into the very fabric of the story and to do so subliminally, so that it bypasses the rational mind and heads straight to the heart, where it is taken up subtly and by inference—in the same way that healing drugs may be administered through salves or skin patches rather than taken orally or by injection. And it is from this coordinated action of subtle communication that the name "*thematic imprinting*" is born.

## PROPOSITIONS

My primary goal in creating *thematic grammar* was to devise a practical means of expressing the *theme* of any story in terms that would apply to any medium, genre, type, or form. Doing so, I imagined, would aid the writer by providing a set of simple rules for identifying and expressing her story *theme*, just as the grammar of equations frees the mathematician to articulate her mathematical ideas.

Because the idea of *thematic grammar* is similar to that of mathematics, it makes sense to look for its roots in that same realm. It also makes sense,

---

[*] Esperanto is a constructed language the rules of which were published in 1887 by its inventor, Dr. L.L. Zamenhof. It boasts only 16 grammatical rules and by some reports is used by over two million people worldwide. Only two feature-length films have ever been made entirely in Esperanto—*Angoroj* [*Agonies*] (1964) and *Incubus* (1965), starring William Shatner, which, if you have never seen it, you absolutely should... just to be able to say that you really have.

however, to use great caution when doing so. The point of the undertaking, after all, is not to pretend that story *themes* can be cast as mathematical equations; they cannot. The point is simply to steal from mathematics the notion that complex assertions can be expressed simply and proven right or wrong. This same notion could be stolen, of course, from any realm of science or law, but mathematics is especially well-suited to the purpose, because it is governed by a language with hard-and-fast rules.

If we apply this notion to storytelling, we may say that the *theme* of any story can be thought of as a *proposition* (definitive statement) that the writer asserts to be true—for example, that one should embrace change when the need to do so arises or should not put all her eggs in one basket. But we-the-audience are not required to accept the *proposition* at face value; rather, we want to see and weigh the evidence for ourselves, so we can draw our own conclusions at the end. The evidence is served up by the story itself—through its characters, their various *intents* and actions, and the manner in which the story unfolds and concludes. And the judgment is handed down by the audience when the book closes, the actors take their bows, the audio track reaches its end, or the credits roll.

Because the *proposition* represents the statement to be supported by the story, it stands at the very heart of the story *theme*. Consequently, it is necessary to be completely clear in its expression. And if it can be expressed in general terms, those terms must be flexible and robust. They must also use precise language, so that they can be applied consistently across all story types, genres, and forms—and their language must be readily customizable. And to fill the bill completely, they must meet and wed (or at least have a torrid affair with) the *grok approach* outlined in Part One.

Oh, and they should be fairly easy to learn.

Is that a tall order? Absolutely. Too tall to be filled? Not at all. In fact, when the smoke of this section clears, it is exactly what we will have done.[*]

## Starting from the Two Basic Forms of Advice

To develop a broad and usable manner of expressing a *proposition*, we begin where our groundwork left off—that is, with the notion that the *theme* of a story can be thought of as advice passed on from one friend to another and that the advice is generally offered in one of two forms:

- You should…
- You should not…

It is from these two nascent forms that we will derive a pair of generic *propositions* that can be tailored to fit any story regardless of *theme*.

---

[*] You are free, of course, to skip this derivation and go straight to the final results on page 92. The idea of *propositions* will make a lot more sense, though, if you know how they are derived, and you'll miss out on some pretty good insight along the way. Just saying.

## Invoking Courses of Action

As a first step in deriving our generic *propositions*, we associate their basic forms with specific *courses of action*, by which I mean matters of doing to which they apply—for example:

- You should break up with your girlfriend.
- You should not trust in voodoo to cure your cancer.

Such pieces of advice are direct, which is good, and each might serve as the basis for an interesting story. The first case, for example, might apply to a boy whose girlfriend is unfaithful or abusive. The second might involve a woman whose devotion to alternative religion is challenged by the onset of disease. And each involves a specific *course of action*, which helps to generate movement in the story.

To generalize them, so that they can be applied to any story, we must state them in versatile, fill-in-the-blank terms that render them universal. Doing so, it turns out, requires nothing more than replacing their specific matters of doing with the phrase *"course of action"* thus:

- You should [*course of action*].
- You should not [*course of action*].

where [*course of action*] is the matter of doing addressed by the statement at hand—in this case, breaking up with your girlfriend or trusting in voodoo to cure your cancer.

As trivial as this maneuver may seem at first glance, it sets the stage for stating *propositions* in a manner that is both all-embracing and personal—so that the *theme* of the story may speak to a broad audience while at the same time retaining the between-you-and-me intimacy of its advice. And it trans our nascent forms into full-fledged first drafts of our generic *propositions*.

## Focusing on the Attempt

Having outfitted our generic *propositions* with *courses of action*, we must distinguish between *courses of action* that involve mere "doing" and those that involve *"attempts* at doing." The difference determines the substance of the *course of action* itself and dictates whether it is suitable for use in a *proposition*. And perhaps not surprisingly, the difference comes down to *intent*. Specifically:

- Activities that involve mere doing do not require *intent*.
- Activities that involve *attempts* at doing do require *intent*.

Closing a bedroom door involves activity, to be sure, but might or might not involve *intent*. The same can be said of crossing a busy city street. But closing the door quietly in an *attempt* not to be heard involves the *intent* to be secretive or at least unobtrusive—which thereby imbues the activity with importance. And the same goes for crossing a street hastily in an *attempt* to reach a parking meter before an approaching meter maid discovers that its time has expired.

In both cases, the critical factor is the absence or presence of *intent*. And it is here that the *grok approach* begins to shake hands with *thematic imprinting*, because the factor revealed by the *grok approach* to be vital to any story (*intent*) turns out to be fundamental to *thematic grammar*, too. In fact, it is this common factor that allows the writer to link the *intent* of her *main character* directly to the story *theme* and thereby cue the music for their wedding march.

When we add "*attempt*" to our generic *propositions*, they become:

- You should *attempt* to [*course of action*].
- You should not *attempt* to [*course of action*].

For example:

- You should *attempt* to break up with your girlfriend.
- You should not *attempt* to trust in voodoo to cure your cancer.

In each case, the *course of action* involves an *attempt* the *success* or *failure* of which is not assured at the outset. And it is the playing out of the *attempt* that drives the plot as the story unfolds.

In fact, in the absence of *attempt*, there is no story. Why? Because the *outcome* is either nonexistent (there is no *goal*) or is completely guaranteed. A story with no *goal* is uninteresting, and one with a guaranteed *outcome* is boring. We-the-audience invest our attention in the story for the specific purpose of watching the characters *attempt* to accomplish their *goals*— uncertain every step of the way of whether they will *succeed*. It is necessary and right, therefore, to include *attempt* in our pair of generic *propositions*. In fact, they would be gapingly incomplete without it.

The inclusion of *attempt* also helps define the *intent* itself. For example, the advice:

- You should not *attempt* to bother a sleeping lion.

is not the same as:

- You should *attempt* to not bother a sleeping lion.

The first might be given to a prankster who has set his sights on pestering a lion at the zoo. The second applies to the poor sap assigned to feed the lion. The *intents* of these two actions differ greatly, and the playing out of their *attempts* will result in two very different scenes.

## Adding the Rationale

Unless a piece of advice comes down from on high by way of a cult leader, fortune cookie, or burning bush, it is entirely reasonable for the advice-recipient to press the giver for justification and to thereby learn the *why* of the advice. In the cases mentioned above, for example, the recipient might ask, "*Why* should I *attempt* to break up with my girlfriend?" or "*Why* should I not *attempt* to trust in voodoo to cure my cancer?"

And unless the advice stems from a drug-induced vision or psychotic episode, it is likely to be associated with a specific *rationale* that appeals to the well-being of the recipient and/or others in her world; otherwise, it would not be offered in the first place. Even compulsive busybodies who feel driven to comment on every situation that crosses their paths (and we all know some of those) tend to justify their advice according to specific *rationales*. For example:

- You should *attempt* to break up with your girlfriend, because she does not understand you.

- You should not *attempt* to trust in voodoo to cure your cancer, because the cancer might spread unchecked.

each of which involves a significant "because."

It is important to note that, in each case, the *rationale* reflects the view-point of the advice giver and might or might not be shared by anyone else— and that another advice giver might offer very different *rationales* for similar advice. For example:

- You should *attempt* to break up with your girlfriend, because she is a cannibal who plans to kill and eat you.

- You should not *attempt* to trust in voodoo to cure your cancer, because the voodoo gods will demand your eternal soul.

The *courses of action* in these two cases are identical to those above, but the natures of the advice differ markedly. And the differences lie entirely in the viewpoints of the advice giver, whose right it is to justify her advices however she likes. In the same respect, it is the absolute right of the writer to determine the *rationale* behind the advice contained in her *theme* and to thereby tailor the *theme* to her tastes and beliefs.

Because the *theme* of any story represents the opinion of its writer regarding how to live, it is appropriate and necessary to incorporate the notion of "*rationale*" into our generic *propositions*. And when we do so, they become:

- You should *attempt* to [*course of action*], because [*rationale*].

- You should not *attempt* to [*course of action*], because [*rationale*].

where [*rationale*] is the fill-in-the-blank reasoning behind the advice.

In both of these cases, the addition of the *rationale* transforms the *proposition* from an assertion made without justification to one backed up by reasoned thought. This is progress, but to fully explore the subject of *rationales*, we must examine three aspects of their natures: their types (*conditions* or *consequences*); the *outcomes* from which they spring (*success* or *failure*); and their ultimate results (*rewards* or *harms*).

## Conditions versus Consequences

If we look closely at the *rationales* in our examples above, we notice that they can be grouped into two basic types—*conditions* and *consequences*. For example, in the cases of:

- You should *attempt* to break up with your girlfriend, because she does not understand you.
- You should not *attempt* to trust in voodoo to cure your cancer, because the cancer might spread unchecked.

the first *rationale* appeals to an existing *condition* ("she does not understand you"), and the second appeals to the *consequence* of an *attempted course of action* ("the cancer might spread unchecked").

Is one type superior to the other? Yes, the *consequence*. Why? Because it is directly linked to the *course of action*, and it is the *course of action* that keeps the audience engaged as the story unfolds. A *rationale* based on a *condition* contains no promise or threat regarding what might arise from the *attempted course of action*. A *rationale* based on a *consequence* spells out the potential results of the *attempt*.

To be worthy of inclusion in a *proposition*, therefore, the *rationale* must be expressed in terms of a *consequence*, not a *condition*. And doing so involves more than rewording; it requires the writer to think in explicit terms regarding her characters and their actions, and it rewards her with clarity regarding their ultimate *goals*.

If we apply this concept to the girlfriend advice, for example, we may transform its *condition* into a *consequence* to obtain:

- You should *attempt* to break up with your girlfriend, because you might free yourself to find someone who understands you.

In this case, the statement involves a promise of potential reward ("you might free yourself to find someone who understands you") rather than a mere observation ("she does not understand you"). The promise of reward leads to motivated action, which in turn gives us-the-audience something to watch and a means by which to gauge story progress.

It behooves us, therefore, to express each *rationale* in terms of the "*consequence of the attempt*" that might arise from the *course of action*. And when we do so, our pair of generic *propositions* becomes:

- You should *attempt* to [*course of action*], because [*consequence of the attempt*].

- You should not *attempt* to [*course of action*], because [*consequence of the attempt*].

More progress still. But to state the *consequences* fully, we must take into account the *outcomes* from which they arise—*success* or *failure*.

## Success versus Failure

In each of the statements presented above, the *consequence of the attempt* is expressed in terms of what *might* happen. In the first case, the advice-recipient *might* find someone who understands him. In the second, the cancer *might* spread unchecked. In both cases, however, the *consequence* is based strictly on *success in the attempt*—either to break up with the girlfriend or to trust in voodoo to heal the cancer.

But should all such statements be based on *success in the attempt?* The answer is "yes," and here's why.

It makes no sense to advise someone to *attempt* a *course of action* based on the prospect of what will happen if she *fails*. If I recommend a *course of action* to someone I care about, I am naturally inclined to hope that she *succeeds* in the *attempt* to pursue it. Likewise, if I warn someone against a *course of action*, I am unlikely to base my warning on what will happen if she *fails*. It makes sense for me to say, for example:

- You should *attempt* to break up with your girlfriend, because you might free yourself to find someone who understands you.

but it makes absolutely no sense for me to say:

- You should *attempt* to break up with your girlfriend, because you might remain stuck with someone who does not understand you.

which is the likely outcome if the *attempt* at the breakup *fails*.

And yes, I might recommend breaking up with the girlfriend based on the benefits of even making the *attempt* or the harms that might come from not doing so. But *propositions* in *thematic grammar* are based on *success in the attempt* itself, not on whether the *attempt* is made. We-the-audience invest our attention in the story to watch what the characters do, not what they do not do.

"But what if," you might ask, "I am telling a story about a *main character* who is opposed to *attempting* a *course of action* that his friends consider necessary for his survival—for example, being treated for cancer? Doesn't the story revolve around whether he *succeeds* in even making the *attempt?*"

No, it does not.

If your *main character* is actively opposed to a *course of action* that his friends are advising him to undertake, then he is a *keep* character whose *treasure* is the stand he has taken to ignore their advice. His true *course of action* in the story, therefore, concerns maintaining his stand (to not take their advice) and has nothing to do with the *course of action* that his friends are recommending (being treated for cancer). Strictly speaking, if he *succeeds* in the *attempt* of his *course of action*, his cancer will go untreated. And if his friends are correct that the treatment is required for his survival, then... well, I'm sorry, but he is doomed.

In fact, if we-the-audience support the idea that it would be better for him to undergo treatment, then we will root for him to *fail* in his *attempt* to not take the advice. In that case, the story revolves around an *attempt* we would like to see *fail*—a type of story that I will address in Chapter 10.

For the time being, though, we may simply leave it at this—that to be of practical use in stating a *theme*, a *proposition* must always be expressed in terms of "*success in the attempt.*" To do so, we refine the wording thus:

- You should *attempt* to [*course of action*], because if you *succeed in the attempt*, [*consequence of success*].
- You should not *attempt* to [*course of action*], because if you *succeed in the attempt*, [*consequence of success*].

For example:

- You should *attempt* to break up with your girlfriend, because if you *succeed in the attempt*, you will free yourself to find someone who understands you.
- You should not *attempt* to trust in voodoo to cure your cancer, because if you *succeed in the attempt*, the cancer will spread unchecked.

It is important to note that, in each of these cases, the *consequence* is stated in terms of what *will* happen rather than what *might* happen. And even though this may seem like a minor change in wording, it amplifies the force of the *propositions*. How so? By allowing them to state in unequivocal terms the results of *success in the attempt*.

If I *succeed in the attempt* to close the bedroom door quietly, I will maintain the stealth that, for whatever reason, is of value to me. If I *succeed in the attempt* to reach the parking meter before the meter maid arrives, I will save myself the cost and aggravation of the ticket. These are simplistic examples, to be sure, but they illustrate the importance of "*success in the attempt*" and its power to plant a confident statement at the core of a story *theme*.

Does this mean, by the way, that we can simply ignore the prospect of *failure* when it comes to *thematic grammar?* No, it most certainly does not. It means only that *failure* must be handled in some other way. Fortunately, *thematic imprinting* provides a straightforward means for doing so—by honoring the possibility of *failure* as an *outcome* in the story and establishing its effect on the story *theme* (see Chapter 10).

## Consequences versus Rewards and Harms

Our generic *propositions* address two distinct types of *courses of action*—those that are *advisable* ("You should") and those that are *inadvisable* ("You should not"). And as we have seen, both types base their *consequences* on *success in the attempt.* To distinguish more clearly between them, however, and thereby stress the importance of their advices, we must pronounce judgment on the effects of their respective *consequences* and customize their wording accordingly. And when we do so, we get:

- You should *attempt* to [*course of action*], because if you *succeed in the attempt,* [*reward of success*].

- You should not *attempt* to [*course of action*], because if you *succeed in the attempt,* [*harm of success*].

where [*reward of success*] is the desirable *consequence* of *success* in an *advisable course of action,* and [*harm of success*] is the undesirable *consequence* of *success* in an *inadvisable course of action.*

But does it make sense to speak of a *"harm of success"*? Oh, yes, without question, it does. For example, if a mother *attempts* to ignore the conflicts that brew within her family, then *success in the attempt* might cause them to fester until they explode, leaving the family in shambles. And if a serial killer *attempts* to set a tri-county record for gruesome murders, then *success in the attempt* means that innocent people die.

And remember our prankster at the zoo. If he *succeeds in the attempt* to bother the sleeping lion, he gets mauled and possibly eaten for his efforts—which (for him, at least) is clearly a *harm of success.*

## Accounting for the Why and How

So far, we have based our generic *propositions* on *courses of action.* And although doing so acknowledges the importance of action to the *theme,* it is not sufficient to form a complete *proposition.* Why not? Because it does not address two fundamental factors that affect how the story is received by its audience—which are:

- The motivation that prompts the *course of action*
- The methods by which the *course of action* is pursued

In other words, the term *"course of action"* does not by itself address the *why* (motivation) and *how* (methods) of the *attempt.*

As I noted in Part One, we-the-audience receive the story through two simultaneous channels, our heads and our hearts. For us to decide whether and where to invest our sympathies, we need to know not only *what* the *main character* is *attempting* to do but *why* he feels compelled to make the *attempt* and *how* he *intends* to go about it. We may measure story progress by the *course of action* itself, but it is the *why* and *how* of the characters' actions that determine whether we sympathize with them and how we parse and judge story *theme*.

Sometimes the *why* is implicit—for example, in the story of a father *attempting* to find his kidnapped child. Other times, the *why* is not so clear-cut. A young man, for example, might *attempt* to win the heart of a girl so that he can feel complete in their shared love. Or he might do so to get back at another girl by whom he feels jilted. Or he might do so simply to satisfy a selfish desire for sexual conquest. In the first case, we-the-audience are likely to root for his *success* in the *attempt*. In the second case, we might be less likely to do so. And in the third case, we might root for him to *fail*.

Likewise, our sympathies depend, in part, on the *how* of the *attempt*. If the young man *attempts* to win the girl through poetry and noble deeds, we might be very much on his side. If, on the other hand, his *attempt* involves spelling out her name in dead squirrels on her lawn or murdering a rival for her love, we might be less inclined to hope that he *succeeds* in the *attempt*.

In short, for us-the-audience to determine whether or not to grant our sympathies to a character, we must take into account not only his *intended course of action* but also the *why* and *how* of the *attempt*. Consequently, it behooves us to replace the term *"course of action"* with wording that more clearly honors the *why* and *how*. As it happens, the term *"endeavor"* works quite well in this regard, because it conveys a sense of complexity without diminishing the action itself. And when we employ it, our pair of generic *propositions* becomes:

- You should *attempt* to [*endeavor*], because if you *succeed in the attempt*, [*reward of success*].

- You should not *attempt* to [*endeavor*], because if you *succeed in the attempt*, [*harm of success*].

where [*endeavor*] includes not only the *course of action* itself but the motivation that prompts its making and the methods by which it is *attempted*.

Usually, we-the-audience assume that an *advisable course of action* is to be *attempted* with integrity and that an *inadvisable course of action* is to be disapproved of regardless of how the *attempt* is made. Consequently, it is seldom necessary to spell out the *endeavor* in detail. Doing so can prove quite useful to the writer, however, simply because it forces her to think in exact terms regarding the actions of her characters. For example, if we state the *endeavor* in detail for the girlfriend *proposition*, we might obtain:

- You should *attempt* to break up honorably with your girlfriend as a matter of self-respect, because if you *succeed in the attempt*, you will free yourself to find someone who understands you.

where the *how* of the *endeavor* is "honorably" and the *why* is "a matter of self-respect." Likewise, the voodoo *proposition* might be stated:

- You should not *attempt* to trust in voodoo to cure your cancer and deny all modern forms of treatment as a way of honoring your religion, because if you *succeed in the attempt*, the cancer will spread unchecked.

in which case, the *how* is "deny[ing] all modern forms of treatment," and the *why* is "[to honor] your religion."

In both cases, the *why* provides the writer with significant clues regarding the motivation of her *main character*, and the *how* helps to define the story arc. By expressing them in detail, she may gain important insight into both her *main character* and her story.

## Broadening the Scope

The final tweak required to complete our pair of generic *propositions* involves broadening their scope by hiding the "you" that brought us to this point. And we do so not to abandon the idea of *theme* as personal advice but to expand the applicability of their messages—so that they can be presented readily to the world at large. And because the "you" is deeply ingrained in their development, it is implied in every aspect of their expression and does not get lost.

In this sense, the "you" is like a booster rocket that got us into space. And now that we are safely in orbit, we do not need to jettison the rocket— we can simply tuck it away on the side of our spaceship, where it remains with us but unseen. To put it in less metaphorical terms, we can replace the word "you" with the broader term "one." And when we do so, our pair of generic *propositions* becomes:

- One should *attempt* to [*endeavor*], because *success in the attempt* [*reward of success*].

- One should not *attempt* to [*endeavor*], because *success in the attempt* [*harm of success*].

For example, using wording appropriate to the broadened scope, the girlfriend *proposition* might become:

- One should *attempt* to remove himself from a bad relationship, because *success in the attempt* will create the chance of finding true love.

and our voodoo *proposition* might become:

- One should not *attempt* to trust superstitious ritual to cure disease, because *success in the attempt* will lead to ruined health.

The use of the word "one" in both cases requires that the *propositions* be couched in terms of human universals—in this case, the finding of love and seeking of health. Such universalizing not only changes the phrasing of the *propositions*, it exposes the basic component around which the *theme* revolves—that is, its *issue*.

In brief, the *issue* of a story may be thought of as its topic of concern regarding how to live. It is, in essence, the matter to be debated by the story, and the *theme* represents the opinion of the story regarding its *issue*. In the *propositions* above, for example, the respective *issues* are "removing oneself from a bad relationship" and "trusting superstitious ritual to cure disease." And the *theme* of any story based on one of these *propositions* will represent the opinion of the story regarding its *issue*.

Because the *issue* serves as the central *thematic* focus of the story, it may affect all aspects of the story—including its events, characters, and even its setting and background (see Chapter 10).

## Expressing the Final Forms

So here we are at the end of our derivation, having started from the two basic forms of advice and navigated the if-then landscape of *thematic* logic to arrive at our generic *propositions*, which are (restated here):

- One should *attempt* to [*endeavor*], because *success in the attempt* [*reward of success*].
- One should not *attempt* to [*endeavor*], because *success in the attempt* [*harm of success*].

It may seem like a lot of work for not many words. But as with any well-written sentence, it is not the number of words that counts—it's what they mean. And as I will show in sections to follow, one or the other of these generic *propositions* can be used to create, explore, and express the *theme* of any story and can do so in terms that intertwine completely with the *grok approach*, especially with respect to its focus on the *main character* and his *type of intent* and *treasure*.

And that's where things start to get really cool.

## OUTCOMES

For the reasons I cited above, each *proposition* in our final generic pair is expressed in terms of *success in the attempt*. However, as I pointed out, *success* is only one of two possible *outcomes* for any *attempt*—the other being *failure*. And not only does *failure* serve as a possible *outcome* of the *attempt*, its prospect is vital to the telling of the story, because it identifies the result that we-the-audience will either fear or hope for as the story plays out.

Because *success* and *failure* both represent potential *outcomes* for any *endeavor*, the writer can use either one to support her *proposition*; they merely represent different ways of doing so. For example, to support a *proposition* involving an *advisable endeavor*, she can create a scenario in which the *main character* either: a) *succeeds in the attempt* and reaps the *reward of success* or b) *fails in the attempt* and suffers the *harm of failure*. Likewise, to warn against an *inadvisable endeavor*, the *main character* can either: a) *succeed in the attempt* and suffer the *harm of success*, or *fail in the attempt* and reap the *reward of failure*.

It is not at all hard to imagine a *"harm of failure."* The police detective who *fails* in his *attempt* to capture a killer leaves the killer free to kill again. And the survivor of a plane crash who *fails* in his *attempt* to reach civilization before the gangrene in his broken leg kills him… dies.

But do stories that involve *"reward of failure"* really exist? You bet they do. And some of them are classic and immortal. In fact, when presenting the *grok approach* in Part One, I made regular reference to two such stories that are both well-known and well-told—*Casablanca* and *A Christmas Carol*.

In *Casablanca*, the *main character*, Rick, has distanced himself from the world of those who actively care about others and has built around himself an emotional fortress. When Ilsa and Victor arrive, he strives to maintain that fortress against the threat that they both represent. His *endeavor*—to *keep* his fortress intact—is one that the storytellers appear to consider *inadvisable*, and we-the-audience are likely to agree. By having Rick *fail in the attempt*, and thereby rejoin the ranks of those who make a positive difference in the world (his *reward of failure*), the storytellers support their *proposition* nicely.

In *A Christmas Carol*, the *main character*, Scrooge, is in a similar bind. He, too, has built or allowed to grow on its own a sturdy internal fortress against human contact and kindness. Like Rick, he is engaged in what the author seems to consider an *inadvisable endeavor*. Unlike Rick, however, whose battleground is largely internal, Scrooge is confronted head-on by four ghosts—his dead partner Marley and three others from the Christmas family. In this case, his *endeavor*—to *keep* his tight-hearted world intact—is spelled out explicitly to the audience. By having him *fail in the attempt* and thereby reap the joy that is his *reward of failure*, the author supports the premise of the story *proposition*—that it is *inadvisable* to *keep* oneself guarded from human kindness.

In this way, the *outcome* serves to express the story *theme*, not by taking part in the *proposition*, but by supporting its premise in the form of measurable results. The *main character succeeds* or *fails* and earns a *reward* or *harm*. And merely by doing so, he argues in support of the story *theme*.

The *outcome* is incapable on its own, however, of fully supporting the *theme*. To do so, it must combine with the audience *reaction*.

## REACTIONS

To express a *theme* fully, the writer must not only present a *proposition* and support its premise with an *outcome*, she must engage our sympathies with the *main character* and his *attempted endeavor*. If she is successful in doing so, we-the-audience will be prone to support her *proposition* and will hope for him either to *succeed* (for an *advisable endeavor*) or *fail* (for an *inadvisable endeavor*) in his *attempt*. In either case, our *reaction* depends entirely on our hopes and can be summed up in one of two ways:

· If the *outcome* matches our hopes, we will feel *pleased*.

· If the *outcome* does not match our hopes, we will feel *disappointed*.

It is this simple pair of *reactions—pleased* and *disappointed*—that provides us-the-audience with the gavel we use to judge and accept (or not) the *proposition* that defines the story *theme*. Either *reaction* may be used in any story, and neither is superior to the other, except when it comes to making the story remain in the mind of the audience.*

In *Whale Rider*, for example, we-the-audience can empathize easily with Paikea and hope that she will *succeed* in her *attempt* to *gain* her proper place in the world. And when she *succeeds in the attempt*, we feel *pleased*. By feeling *pleased* with the *outcome* of the story, we offer implicit approval of the *proposition* that lies at the core of its *theme*—that one should *attempt* to *gain* her proper place in the world, because *success in the attempt* will bring about satisfaction and health for all concerned.

Likewise, in *Casablanca*, we feel *pleased* when Rick *fails in the attempt* to maintain his emotional fortress, and by doing so we support the story *proposition*, that one should not *attempt* to isolate himself from actively caring for others. In *Chinatown*, on the other hand, we feel *disappointed* when private detective Jake Gittes *fails in the attempt* to expose and bring to justice the man behind the murder of Hollis Mulray. But by feeling *disappointed* in his failure, we demonstrate our agreement with the story *proposition*—that one should *attempt* to find and expose the perpetrators of crime and injustice.

These stories illustrate an important point about *thematic imprinting*— that the audience *reaction* does not depend on whether an *endeavor* is *advisable* or *inadvisable* or the *outcome* of its *attempt* involves *success* or *failure*. The *reaction* depends, instead, on how the two are combined. Specifically:

---

* Stories that leave the audience *disappointed* (in the *outcome*, not the storytelling) tend to stick longer in its mind—simply because it is easier to let go of a story that has been neatly wrapped up with a pleasing conclusion than it is a story with an *outcome* we would like to see changed.

| *endeavor* Type | + | *outcome* | = | *reaction* |
|:---:|:---:|:---:|:---:|:---:|
| *advisable* | + | *success* | = | *pleased* |
| *advisable* | + | *failure* | = | *disappointed* |
| *inadvisable* | + | *success* | = | *disappointed* |
| *inadvisable* | + | *failure* | = | *pleased* |

As we will see in Chapter 10, this quartet of combinations can prove extraordinarily useful in examining existing stories for their commonalities and for exploring the expression of *theme* in stories under development.

## ANOTHER NUTSHELL AND EXAMPLE

Okay, so to put things in yet another small nutshell, the foundations of *thematic imprinting* are based on three elements of *thematic grammar*:

- *Proposition*
- *Outcome*
- *Reaction*

The *proposition* is the statement made by the story regarding how to live. The *outcome* is the *succeed*-or-*fail* result of an *attempted endeavor* contained in the *proposition*. The *reaction* is the expected *pleased*-or-*disappointed* response of the audience upon witnessing the *outcome* of the *attempt*.

As an example of how all three work together to express a story *theme*, consider a story in which a young man *attempts* to make friends in a foreign land—perhaps a new school or city or distant country. And let us assume that the writer is in favor of the idea and that she bases her opinion on the emotional wellness that friendship provides. In this case, the *issue* is "making friends in a foreign land," and the *proposition* might take the form:

- One should *attempt* to make friends in a foreign land, because *success in the attempt* will lead to the emotional wellness that friendship provides.

which is sound advice with which most people might agree.

If the young man *succeeds in the attempt* and reaps the emotional wellness referred to in the *proposition*, it is likely that we-the-audience will feel *pleased* at the *outcome*. If, on the other hand, he *fails in the attempt* and commits suicide because his loneliness overwhelms him, we-the-audience will probably feel *disappointed*. In either case, however, the writer will have supported the *proposition* in her story—that one should *attempt* to make friends in a foreign land. She will simply have used a different *outcome* to do it.

The first *outcome* results in a feel-good story that leaves us-the-audience feeling *pleased*; the second case is a depressing story that leaves us *disappointed* (at the *outcome*, not the story itself). But the *thematic declaration* is the same in both cases. The difference between them lies strictly in the *outcome* of the *attempt* and its impact on how we-the-audience feel when it is revealed.

It is this ability to express a story *theme* by means of a *main character* who *attempts* an *endeavor* and *succeeds* or *fails* in the *attempt* that constitutes the elegant simplicity of *thematic imprinting* and imbues it with power and storytelling magic. And let's face it... the magical engagement of an audience for its delight and enlightenment is the precious brass ring for which all great writers strive.

# Chapter 10

## USING THEMATIC GRAMMAR

Now, it gets fun.

Having derived the three basic elements of *thematic grammar* and established how they combine to express a story *theme*, we find ourselves in position, at last, to close the philosophical loop of this entire enterprise by exploring the link that connects *thematic imprinting* to the *grok approach*. We do not need to construct the link; we need only to recognize its existence. In fact, I referred to the link in Chapter 9 when addressing the importance of *attempt*.

Simply put, the link is *intent*.

To realize its importance, we must examine its nature and use, not only with respect to *propositions* and their *endeavors* but with regard to the *issue* that burns at the heart of the story *theme* and the magical symbiosis between *outcomes* and *reactions* and how they combine to express that *theme*.

## UNDERSTANDING AND USING INTENT

As I demonstrated in Part One, it is the *intent* of the *main character* that moves the story forward and supports the very foundations of the story. In simple terms, the *intent* serves three primary functions, which are:

- generating concrete, purposeful action on the part of the *main character*,
- providing the standard against which story progress is measured, and
- creating an *endeavor* that serves as the foundation of the story *theme*.

It is these three functions that render *intent* essential to the creation of a compelling story, which is why the *grok approach* employs it as a foundational component—specifically the idea that the motivation of any character can be expressed in terms of one of three *types of intent*. To:

- *gain* a *treasure* that he has never possessed,
- *regain* a *treasure* that he previously possessed, or
- *keep* a *treasure* that he currently possesses.

But *intent* is essential to *thematic imprinting*, too. It is, in fact, the magic dust that transforms a *course of action* from mere "doing" into an "*attempt* at doing" and thereby renders it suitable for use in a *proposition*.

Given the critical role of *intent* in both the *grok approach* and *thematic imprinting*, it is reasonable to conclude that it could serve as a bridge between the two. And perhaps even more than a bridge—maybe a link that unites them to create a unified whole, like a storytelling Ouroboros*.

But can one really make use of this link? The answer is "yes," and here's how—by stating the *endeavor* in terms of a *type of intent*. And doing so not only uses the link, it forces one to search for its *whys* and *hows*, by which I mean to examine the story for its motivations (*whys*) and methods (*hows*). And because the examination is guided by a specific purpose, it can provide deep insights for the writer, enriching her understanding of the story under development and helping to render its characters lively and whole.

## EXPRESSING THE ENDEAVOR IN *grok* TERMS

To link the *grok approach* directly to the *theme* of her story, the writer must think of the *endeavor* in terms of a *type of intent*. Take, for example, our young man seeking friends in a foreign land, the *proposition* of whose story we expressed as:

- One should *attempt* to make friends in a foreign land, because *success in the attempt* will lead to the emotional wellness that friendship provides.

In this case, the *advisable endeavor* involves the *attempt* of the *main character* to make friends in a foreign land. But if we couch the matter in *grok* terms, we may describe him as a *gain* character whose *treasure* is the friendship he *intends* to make. When stated in these terms, the *proposition* becomes:

- One should *attempt* to *gain* friends in a foreign land, because *success in the attempt* will lead to the emotional wellness that friendship provides.

By making this minor change to the wording, we are using *grok* terminology to state plainly that the friendship the young man seeks is a *treasure* that he has never before possessed (at least in the foreign land). If, in another story, he possessed friendship at one time and suffered its loss, maybe by taking it for granted, then he would be a *regain* character *attempting* to recapture the friendship he once knew—in which case, the *proposition* might be stated:

---

* Ouroboros is an ancient symbol of a serpent biting its own tail and thereby creating a circle. It has been used throughout history—for example, to represent Kundalini energy (India), the Aztec god Quetzalcoatl, the serpent Jörmungandr (Norse mythology), and the first living thing in the universe (by Plato). It is also used in the seal of Theosophy, whose motto is, "There is no religion higher than truth." And the chemist August Kekulé (1829–1896) is said to have credited a dream of Ouroboros with his discovery of the structure of benzene. So there's that.

- One should *attempt* to *regain* lost friendship, because *success in the attempt* will restore the emotional wellness that friendship provides.

Both stories advocate the seeking of friendship as an *advisable endeavor*, they simply take different approaches to doing so. And each may differ from the other in many details. In the first scenario, for example, the *main character* might need to learn where and how to look for friendship and how to secure it when it appears. In the second, he might need to make amends with old friends or seek out new friends while being careful not to repeat his past mistakes.

In either case, the stating of the *endeavor* in terms of its *type of intent* automatically links the *grok approach* to the *theme* of the story by spelling out the standards that we-the-audience will use to gauge progress and react to the *outcome*. Specifically, we will measure story progress in terms of the *intent* of the *main character* to achieve his *goal*, and we will judge that *intent* when reacting to the *outcome*, thereby parsing the story *theme*. In this way, the *grok approach* and *thematic imprinting* work hand-in-hand to create the complete story experience for us-the-audience—to draw us into its confidences and send us off when the story is over with its message whispered into our souls.

## FINDING AND EXPRESSING THE INTENT

To establish an organic link between the *type of intent* and story *theme*, the writer must examine the *intent* of her *main character* to ensure that it is both accurate and well-suited for use in a *proposition*. And to do so, she must think in the large with respect to its expression and in detail with regard to the *endeavor* involved.

## Thinking in the Large

Because the *proposition* applies to human experience in the large, the *intent* at the heart of its *endeavor* must be expressed in broad terms—for example, "to *gain* friendship," rather than in specific terms such as "to *gain* the good graces of that girl with the gorgeous hair." This broad form of expression allows the *theme* to speak to human universals.

Although the *main character* must possess an *outer goal* to pursue and hold as a standard of measure (for himself and us-the-audience) regarding whether or not he *succeeds*, it is the broadly stated *inner goal* that expresses the story *theme*. In the case of our displaced young man, for example, his *outer goal* might take the form of an invitation to join a bowling team or the offer to take part in a blood sacrifice. But what matters with regard to the *theme* is whether he *gains* (or *regains*) friendship, not the form in which it may appear. The bowling invitation and blood-sacrifice offer, in this case, are merely tokens that indicate his *success* or *failure* in doing so.

## Thinking in Detail

To construct the *proposition* best suited to her story, the writer must dig deep into the soul of her *main character* and examine in detail the *intent* that lies at the heart of his *endeavor*. And to do so, she must consider the motivations (*whys*) and methods (*hows*) of his *attempt*.

As an example of such digging, consider a story in which a father urges his teenage daughter to excel at high school gymnastics. Does he do so in an *attempt* to impart to her (*gain* in her) a respect for a family ethic? Or does he hope to *gain* for himself a sense of status among his peers? And does he pursue his *goal* with positive reinforcement by encouraging her to work hard and helping wherever he can? Or does he berate her, run her ragged with practice, and impose unreasonable restrictions on her diet and social life?

These are the *whys* and *hows* that must be taken into account when developing the *proposition* of the story, and each plays a vital role in both the *advisability* of the *endeavor* and the nature of its *intent*. In the case of the father and daughter, for example, the *proposition* might take the form:

- One should *attempt* to instill (*gain*) in his children a respect for hard work by assisting them in positive ways, because *success in the attempt* will equip them to do well in life and preserve the work ethic itself.

or, conversely:

- One should not *attempt* to exploit his children to *gain* status for himself, because *success in the attempt* will turn them against him and render the status worthless.

Either of these *propositions* could serve as the basis for a rich and meaningful story, and neither is superior to the other. Their differences lie only in the stories and *themes* that result from their use.* By choosing one over the other, or constructing an alternative to both, the writer can express the opinion most important to her regarding how to live.

# IDENTIFYING AND WORKING WITH ISSUES

As I noted in Chapter 9, every *proposition* revolves around an *issue* that may be thought of as a topic of concern about how to live. And the *theme* represents the opinion of the story regarding its *issue*. The *issue*, therefore, permeates the story—so much so that it colors every character and serves as the partial focus of every scene.

---

* Note, too, that each of these *propositions* could be further broadened by replacing the term "your children" with "those under your influence," which expands the spectrum of stories that can be told to support the *proposition* and thereby renders the *theme* even broader in scope.

In *Casablanca*, for example, the story may be said to revolve around the *issue* of "guarding oneself from caring about others," which is the state in which we find Rick when the story begins. In *Whale Rider*, the *issue* is, "defying tradition to seek your place in the world." And in *Four Weddings and a Funeral*, the *issue* of "finding your soul mate" consumes its *main character*, Charles, throughout the film.

To examine the matter of *issues* and their importance in telling stories, one must look at the manner in which characters serve as arguments for or against them. It is also worthwhile to consider how to look for and refine an *issue* and how to identify an *issue* in a story already underway.

## CHARACTERS AS ARGUMENTS FOR/AGAINST ISSUES

The *issue* at the heart of any story may be said to provide the underlying drive for its characters' actions—not only those of the *main character*, but those of the other characters, as well. By his or her behavior, each character shines a light on the *issue*, thereby illuminating it from an important angle and offering an argument on one of its many sides. And each illumination reveals some small-but-significant aspect of the *issue*—the assembled collection of which informs the *theme*.

In *Casablanca*, for example, Rick represents the idea that "guarding oneself from caring about others" is the basis of an *inadvisable endeavor*. His position on the *issue* is supported by Captain Renault, who takes a neutral stance toward the Nazis and refuses to get involved in the politics of the times. It is staunchly opposed, however, by Ilsa and Victor, both of whom may be said to serve as arguments for active caring. And even the petty crook Ugarte casts light on the *issue*, simply because he appeals to Rick to come to his own salvation when he is arrested—which Rick does not.

In *Whale Rider*, Paikea embodies the notion that "defying tradition to attain your proper place in the world" constitutes an *advisable endeavor*. Her grandfather, Koro, on the other hand, represents the opposing idea—arguing by his attitude and actions that tradition trumps destiny at all costs. But even Paikea's father, Porourangi, may be viewed in terms of the stand he takes on the *issue*—simply by virtue of his own defiance of Koro and his flight from his tribal roots to pursue his own place as an artist elsewhere in the world. And, of course, the tribal origin myth is rife with references to both destiny and tradition.

And in *Four Weddings and a Funeral*, the *main character*, Charles, represents the idea that "finding your soul mate" is well worth *attempting* to do. When we meet him, he has dated many women (and attached himself to none), but not in the shallow quest for selfish adventure. He is not a braggart or lothario. And when he delivers his best-man toast at the very first wedding, he confesses heartfelt envy for those who find and commit to one person, thereby giving voice to a personal desire.

Other characters in the story represent alternative views about "finding your soul mate." Charles' friend Fiona, for example, represents the supporting view, because behind her high-brow cynicism lies the long-held feeling that Charles is "the one" for her. Likewise, the death of their mutual friend Gareth exposes the deep love between him and his partner, Matthew—and again supports the idea that soul mates exist and are worth seeking. Charles' wealthy, inept friend Tom, on the other hand, represents the opposing view, not because he is against the idea of soul mates, but because he believes that simple companionship constitutes a sufficient ideal. The opposing view is also represented by Henrietta, the girl whom Charles makes plans to marry after Carrie (the true object of his desire) becomes out of reach. And the very existence of Henrietta represents the compromise that results from abandoning the search.

## HARVESTING ISSUES

The mere recognition that an *issue* hides at the heart of the *proposition* provides a powerful tool that the writer may use to probe the depths of her *theme*. And its usefulness derives, in part, from the multitude of *issues* that are available to her as starting points—for example: taking revenge, defying unjust authority, or keeping secrets.

*Issues* such as these may derive from the personal concerns of the writer herself, of course, but they can also be harvested elsewhere, especially in works that address any form of human behavior, such as those found in the realms of religion, philosophy, psychology[*], and even evolutionary science[†]. But wherever they are found, they often constitute rich sources of *issues* from which wonderful stories can be built. And using them requires nothing more than examining the referred-to behavior in light of the *grok approach* and extracting from it an *endeavor* that can serve as the expression of an *issue* (pro or con).

A religious reference to forgiveness, for example, can be *issue*-ized by couching it in terms of "forgiving one who has wronged you" or "obtaining forgiveness for your sins." Either *issue* could serve as the core of a wonderful story, but the stories could differ from each other in nearly every way. Likewise, a cultural reference to respect owed to elders, could be *issue*-ized to "respecting your elders" or "demanding respect from the young," either of which could serve as the *thematic* foundation for a story.

Regardless of the source of the *issue*, however, the writer is completely free to promote, disregard, or discredit the position, advice, or conclusions

---

[*] See, for example, Abraham H. Maslow, *Motivation and Personality, Third Edition* (Harper & Row Publishers, Inc., 1970).

[†] See Michael Shermer, *The Science of Good and Evil: Why People Cheat, Gossip, Care, Share, and Follow the Golden Rule* (Holt Paperbacks, 2004)—especially *Appendix II: Moral and Religious Universals as a Subset of Human Universals.*

that derive from the source itself. The purpose of the search is to identify possible *issues* to use in a story—*not* to promote or condemn the original source. As I noted above, the *issue* is the matter up for debate, and the *theme* is the opinion of the story regarding the *issue*. And because the writer enjoys the complete and rightful freedom to let the story reflect (or not) her personal biases, she is at liberty to convert any *issue* to a *theme* in any manner she likes.

## REFINING AN ISSUE

Any *issue* stated in the manner described above can serve as the valid core of a *proposition*. To be suitable for use in an *endeavor*, however, the *issue* must include some acknowledgment of the *why* and *how*. In *Whale Rider*, for example, the *issue* is not simply "attaining your proper place in the world," it is "defying tradition to attain your proper place in the world." Likewise, in the film *The Player* (examined below) the *issue* is not simply "retaining your status"; it is "abandoning moral behavior to retain your status." In both of these cases, the *issue* addresses the motivation and/or manner in which its *endeavor* itself is *attempted*. Such refinements impart specificity to the *issue* and help to focus the story *theme*.

## IDENTIFYING THE ISSUE IN A STORY

Because the *issue* plays a critical role in defining the story *theme*, the writer is well-advised to spot it early on, so that she can blend it fully into her story. As I noted above, she can harvest and select the *issue* even before development begins, in which case it becomes ingrained in the story from the outset and seeps into its very foundations. But what about a story that is already in the works—one that has squirted out of its birth canal and is learning to crawl on the page? Does it have a hidden *issue* somewhere, and can that *issue* be found?

The answer is "yes" on both counts. And to do so, the writer needs simply to examine two of its fundamental facets:

- The characters who populate its world
- The *inciting incident* that starts its motor running

## Examining the Characters

As I noted above, the characters in a fully developed story tend to represent points of view on various sides of an *issue*. It follows, then, that the writer may look to her characters for clues regarding any yet-undiscovered *issue* in a story on which she is working. By examining their actions and behaviors, she may be able to discern a single matter of importance that is common to them all. And that matter may well constitute the *issue* of the story (but might need a little tweaking to take the proper form).

When examining the characters in this manner, of course, the *main character* is more likely than any other to serve as the mother lode. It is his story that we-the-audience will watch, after all, and the roots of the *issue* are sure to be found in his *treasure* and *intent*.

## Examining the Inciting Incident

Every story contains some form of *inciting incident* that starts its motor, usually by imparting to the *main character* the *intent* that motivates him and provides the spine of the story. The *inciting incident* may take place somewhere in Act I or even before we-the-audience strap ourselves in for the ride. Regardless of its location, however, it contains important clues that can be used to determine the *issue* of the story.

In some stories, the *issue* lies naked and exposed at the scene of the *inciting incident*. In *Four Weddings and a Funeral*, for example, the *issue* of "finding your soul mate" leaves its fingerprints all over the scene in which Carrie walks into the church where Charles is serving as best man at the first wedding—and manifests in the devastating thrill of love at first sight... the unconscious connection required for the mating of souls. In *Whale Rider*, the *issue* of "defying tradition to attain your proper place in the world" permeates the opening scene in which Paikea is born and her mother and twin brother die—leaving her grandfather without a viable candidate for leader and prompting her father to defiantly grant her a sacred name. And in *Casablanca*, the *issue* of "guarding oneself against caring for others" steps into the spotlight as soon as Ilsa and Victor walk in the door.

Regardless of whether the *inciting incident* announces itself in the thunderous blast of an explosion triggered by bank robbers or the delicate subtlety of a woman who accidently spies her husband having a drink with a girl she does not know, the part of the story in which it takes place may be well imagined as a crime scene to be carefully sifted for clues regarding the *issue* that lies there.

# EXPLORING OUTCOMES AND REACTIONS

As I mentioned in Chapter 9, the *outcome* and *reaction* work together to express the story *theme*. Consequently, they must be considered jointly with regard to their study and use. And doing so, it turns out, reveals important insights into the nature of story *themes*.

To recap the matter, the *outcome* of any story can be expressed in either of two forms—*success* or *failure*. And the expected audience *reaction* can be expressed as either *pleased* or *disappointed*, depending on whether the *outcome* matches its hopes. When we define the *outcomes* and *reactions* in this way, we can construct an "*outcome/reaction* quartet" consisting of four categories into which any story can be placed. It looks like this.

| *outcome/reaction* | Description |
|---|---|
| *succeed/pleased* | • *Main character succeeds* in the *attempt* of an *advisable endeavor*<br>• Audience is *pleased* with the *outcome* |
| *succeed/disappointed* | • *Main character succeeds* in the *attempt* of an *inadvisable endeavor*<br>• Audience is *disappointed* in the *outcome* |
| *fail/pleased* | • *Main character fails* in the *attempt* of an *inadvisable endeavor*<br>• Audience is *pleased* with the *outcome* |
| *fail/disappointed* | • *Main character fails* in the *attempt* of an *advisable endeavor*<br>• Audience is *disappointed* in the *outcome* |

When considering these four types, it is important to separate the expected audience *reaction* from its *mood*, by which I mean its assessment of the ending as *happy* or *unhappy*. Although the two often align, they are not required to do so. For example, if a hero *succeeds* in his *attempt* to stop aliens from taking over the world but loses the life of his lover in the process, we-the-audience are likely to be *pleased* at the *outcome* (that the aliens have been defeated) but consider the ending *unhappy*. Likewise, if a detective *fails* to discover the perpetrator of a crime but betters his life in the process of making the *attempt*, we may be *disappointed* in the *outcome* (that the perpetrator escapes justice) but consider the ending *happy*.

To understand the impact of this method of classification, we need merely to examine existing stories to see where they fit in. By doing so, we not only gain insight into the classifications themselves; we reveal important (and heretofore hidden) properties that make certain stories work. And in the process, we set the stage for creating an *"outcome/reaction* table," which we can use to survey the landscape of stories in the large. We also position ourselves to examine two complicating factors—*consolations* and *collateral damage*—that determine whether an ending is truly *happy*.

## EXAMINING EXISTING STORIES

The *outcome/reaction* quartet and its system of classification may be understood best by examining existing stories from each of its four types. Doing so reveals common attributes among stories in each type and suggests ways in which those attributes can help identify particular approaches and solutions that might be of use when developing stories of a similar type.

To render this examination as illuminating as possible, each type listed in the *outcome/reaction* quartet is represented here by two stories, and each of the two stories employs a different *type of intent* for its *main character*.

## Succeed/Pleased Stories

In a *succeed/pleased* story, the *main character succeeds* in the *attempt* of an *advisable endeavor*, and we-the-audience are *pleased* that he does so. Such stories comprise the vast majority of produced and published works, most probably because of their tendency to culminate in crowd-pleasing endings. As I noted above, stories with *"pleased"* *outcomes* do not have *happy* endings by default—but in most cases they do, and they tend to leave the audience feeling satisfied. Two of the many stories that can be reasonably placed in this category are *Whale Rider* and *The Wizard of Oz*.

### *Whale Rider*

In *Whale Rider*, the *main character*, Paikea, is a young Maori girl who feels compelled to play a significant role in the life of her tribe. She is hindered in her efforts by her grandfather, Koro, a traditionalist who feels that she is not suited for such involvement, primarily because she is not male.

Paikea is a *gain* character whose *treasure* is what she feels to be her proper place in the tribe, not necessarily at its head (as her conscious *goal*) but at its heart, where she can honor in positive ways its history and health. The nature of her pursuit involves the fulfillment of personal destiny, not only for her own sake but for that of her people. And because her motives seem to be pure, we-the-audience are likely to side with her and hope that she *succeeds* in her *attempt*.

Since we-the-audience hope for her *success in the attempt*, it may be assumed that the storytellers consider her *endeavor* to be *advisable*. In broad terms, therefore, the *proposition* for *Whale Rider* can be stated as:

- One should *attempt* to *gain* her proper place in the world even at the cost of defying tradition, because *success in the attempt* will result in happiness and health for all concerned.

Although the story is rich with interesting side tales, we-the-audience measure its progress solely by means of Paikea and her quest for involvement in her tribe. At its climax, a tremendous personal sacrifice on her part demonstrates her bravery and proves her worthiness to possess the role she seeks, convincing even Koro that tradition may sometimes be damned and that she may well be suited to leadership after all, despite the obvious fact that she is not male.

Because the story ends with the *success* that we-the-audience hoped for, we are *pleased* with the *outcome*; therefore, *Whale Rider* stands as a shining example of a well-told *succeed/pleased* story.

## The Wizard of Oz

In the *The Wizard of Oz*, young Kansan Dorothy Gale is transported by a tornado from her home on the plains to the weird and wonderful world of the Land of Oz—a magical place filled with strange beings and ruled by a powerful wizard known as Oz. From the moment she lands and learns where she is, Dorothy has one major *intent*—to return to the home from which she has been displaced. And although her journey is not without tangents, and is filled with acts of kindness and perseverance, it is the single-minded *intent* of returning home that drives her actions.

Like Paikea in *Whale Rider*, Dorothy's story revolves around her finding and claiming her proper place in the world. But unlike Paikea, whose proper place is one she has never possessed, Dorothy's journey is one of return—specifically, the *attempt* to *regain* the place she thinks of as home. Consequently, the *proposition* of her story may be rendered as:

- One should *attempt* to *regain* her proper place in the world when displaced by forces outside her control, because *success in the attempt* will restore balance to her life and the world.

Although the resolution of her journey hangs on the fortuitous vulnerability of the Wicked Witch of the West to $H_2O$, it is her dogged perseverance in pursuing her *goal*, and doing so with integrity, that puts her in position to achieve that *goal* and wins our hearts in the process. In the end, she returns to Kansas with a greater appreciation of the home from which she was torn. In short, she *succeeds* in her *attempt* and we-the-audience are *pleased* that she has done so—which makes *The Wizard of Oz* a *succeed/pleased* story.

## Succeed/Disappointed Stories

*Succeed/disappointed* stories are rarer than other types, most likely because their endings tend to leave the audience with the unnerving sense of a sin having gone unpunished. Because the story is carried by the *main character*, we-the-audience grant him the investment of attention, regardless of whether or not we support his *goal*. And if that *goal* is selfish and injurious to others, we root for his *failure* as a way of affirming our intuitive sense that the world is better off when justice is served. If he *succeeds* in getting away with the sin and/or injuring others, he earns our contempt and leaves us *disappointed*. If we could step into the story and expose the scoundrel, we would... and help bring him to justice.

Sometimes the sin is sweeping in scope, like the conquest of a nation or destruction of innocent lives in pursuit of power. Other times, it is small and personal, as soft as the whispered lie that destroys a marriage. Regardless of its magnitude, however, its effect in the story is the same—to create an imbalance of justice that refuses to be set right by the end of the story.

Two stories that fit well in this category are *Swimming with Sharks* and *The Player*. Both involve *main characters* who get away with murder and both are set in the world of Hollywood films. These stories are instructive not only because they provide examples of the *succeed/disappointed* type but because they illustrate the importance of *whys* and *hows* in the *attempt*. Specifically, they demonstrate that the audience judgment transcends the *course of action*—and that it hangs on the methods used and costs to be paid for *success*.

## Swimming with Sharks

In *Swimming with Sharks*, a young screenwriter named Guy goes to work for a Hollywood mogul and is thrilled for the chance to do so, thinking it gives him a foot in one very big door. Soon after he begins his employment, however, he discovers that the mogul is abusive and prone to humiliating those who work around him. And when the mogul takes credit for developing a screenplay Guy has written, Guy breaks into the mogul's home and proceeds to subdue and torture him.

At the climax, Guy faces a choice of whom to murder—the mogul or his own girlfriend, who has come to the mogul's door to pitch a script. The final scene reveals that he has done the latter... and that he has pinned on the girlfriend the break-in and torture of the mogul. In doing so, he has become world-wise in an ugly sense, like the mogul himself. As a result, the *proposition* for *Swimming with Sharks* may be stated:

- One should not *attempt* to *gain* status at the cost of abandoning moral conduct, because *success in the attempt* will render the status hollow and worthy of contempt.

By the time the credits roll, Guy has *succeeded* in his *attempt* to *gain* the status he desires—or at least appears to be well on his way to doing so. But we-the-audience know him to be a murderous villain, and in our minds he has joined the ranks of those who deserve to be jailed. His *success* offends us and leaves us *disappointed*, which renders *Swimming with Sharks* as a *succeed/disappointed* story.

And lest you be tempted to suggest that our condemnation of Guy's hard-won status as hollow carries no weight because we do not really live in his story world, I offer this: We are a social species and tend to rely on the approval of the collective for our sense of well-being. That is why there are morality tales and laws against murder and theft—and why the practice of "shunning" works in many contexts. Some of us cast that approval in the form of religious strictures; others do not. But all of us feel it, and evidence suggests that it may be encoded in our genes. So when we-the-audience shake our fists in denouncement of some kind of conduct, even if the parties involved are not flesh-and-blood persons, we reaffirm the power of the collective in our lives.

By inviting us into the story, the storytellers swear us in as judges of right and wrong. And when we pound our gavel in judgment, the hands of all humanity share in the blows. So yes, it really does matter what we think.

## The Player

In *The Player*, studio executive Griffin Mill begins receiving threatening postcards that he assumes are being sent by a screenwriter whose pitch he once rejected. To put an end to the threats, he seeks out the screenwriter to offer him a scriptwriting deal. In the course of their meeting, a fight ensues and Griffin accidentally kills the screenwriter. From that point forward, he must *keep* secret the fact that he is the killer—while also protecting (*keeping*) his studio job from an up-and-coming story executive and dealing with the ongoing arrival of threatening postcards, whose author he had guessed incorrectly. And every step of the way, he demonstrates an affinity for self-interest and deception.

The *proposition* for *The Player* is similar in essence to that of *Swimming with Sharks* but differs in its *type of intent* and may be stated:

- One should not *attempt* to *keep* his status at the cost of abandoning moral conduct, because *success in the attempt* will render the status hollow and worthy of contempt.

In the end, Griffin *succeeds* in getting away with the murder and retaining the status he sought to *keep* throughout. But as with Guy in *Swimming with Sharks*, his *success* offends our moral sensibilities and leaves us *disappointed*, because justice does not prevail. Consequently, *The Player* is a *succeed/disappointed* story.

## Fail/Pleased Stories

In a *fail/pleased* story, the *main character fails* in his *attempt* to pursue an *endeavor*, and we are *pleased* that he does so. Our pleasure might arise from watching someone whose *endeavor* we oppose be defeated by an opponent we like or from seeing someone we care about *fail* in his *attempt* to pursue an *endeavor* that will lead to his ruin.

Such stories are well-represented by two examples from wildly different genres—*How the Grinch Stole Christmas!* and *Casablanca*.

## How the Grinch Stole Christmas!

In *How the Grinch Stole Christmas!*, the *main character*, Grinch, is a mean creature who cannot stand the joyous sounds that issue at Christmastime from Whoville—a town of innocents that lies at the base of the mountain on which he lives. To prevent the noises from coming one year, he devises a plan to steal the very holiday itself, which he imagines to consist of the trappings of Christmas instead of the spirit that gives them meaning.

To develop a *proposition* for the story, it is necessary to examine closely the nature of his *intent*. We can dismiss, for example, the idea that his *endeavor* involves *regaining*, because as far as we know, he has never not known the noise of Christmas in Whoville—whose exuberant celebrations seem to be a longstanding tradition. Consequently, his *treasure* is not one that he possessed at one time and then lost. Ergo, there is nothing for him to *regain*.

Likewise, we can discard the idea of *keeping* as his *intent*. A *keep* character is satisfied with the state of things as they are and does not act until that state faces a threat. And although the Grinch is free of the noise of Whovillian celebration for 364 days out of the year, he is not at all content with the fact that he lives with the inevitability of its return. So no, he is not a *keep* character, either.

The process of elimination reveals, therefore, that the Grinch is a *gain* character. And it also reveals the *treasure* he hopes to *gain*—a year without Christmas in Whoville.

Having identified his *treasure* and *type of intent*, we can pull back and view the story in the large. And doing so reveals that what he is *attempting* to *gain* may be accurately stated as selfishly getting his way at others' expense. The *proposition* can be stated, therefore:

- One should not *attempt* to *gain* personal satisfaction at the expense of others, because *success in the attempt* will render him worthy of scorn and distrust.

As with the *succeed/disappointed* stories described above, the results of the *outcome* here are judged by us-the-audience using accepted moral norms of proper conduct. Such norms are based on the harms that may be suffered when they are broken—and as such, they represent perfectly valid measures by which we may approach the story *theme*. In this case (and most cases), they also reflect the moral judgment of the storyteller.

In the course of this story, however, the Grinch *fails* in his *attempt* to prevent the arrival of Christmas in Whoville. And not only does it come despite his efforts, its message gets through to him, his heart grows large, and he accepts an invitation to join the Whos in their holiday feast.

So here is a case where the *main character fails* in his *attempt* to pursue an *endeavor* that the storyteller considers *inadvisable*. We-the-audience agree with the storyteller and are *pleased* by the *failure*; therefore, *How the Grinch Stole Christmas!* is a story of the *fail/pleased* type.

## Casablanca

In *Casablanca*, Rick Blaine has abandoned a life of active involvement in human affairs and isolated himself in the world of the nightclub he owns in Casablanca, Morocco. The days when he fought against Fascism with rebels in Spain are behind him—as is a romantic Parisian affair with Ilsa, a beautiful woman whom he loved deeply. Due in part to the emotional devastation caused by her perceived betrayal, he has retreated to the politically neutral world of Casablanca and created for himself an emotional fortress against his own feelings and needs—and those of others.

Although Rick has allowed himself to harden emotionally, he is nevertheless possessed of an honest nobility—an undying remnant of the man he once was. We-the-audience like him and would like to see him let down his guard and re-enter the world of those who care and are cared for. And when Ilsa reappears in his life, along with her freedom-fighter husband, the fortress that Rick has erected comes under attack, and we hope that he will lose the fight, so that he might enjoy the fruits of a healthy life.

We can state the *proposition* for *Casablanca* simply as:

- One should not *attempt* to *keep* himself from caring about others, because *success in the attempt* will deny him the satisfaction and emotional health that caring brings.

By the end of the story, Rick loses the fight to *keep* his emotional fortress intact. We witness the loss in his willingness to give Ilsa and her husband the letters of transit that will allow them to escape Casablanca. He also kills the arrogant Nazi major and forms what appears to be a long-term friendship with the French captain whom he has long considered little more than a bothersome acquaintance. In short, Rick *fails* in his *attempt* to *keep* from caring actively about others, and we-the-audience are *pleased* at his *failure*. Consequently, *Casablanca* stands as a *fail/pleased* story.

## Fail/Disappointed Stories

In a *fail/disappointed* story, the *main character fails* at the *attempt* of an *advisable endeavor*, and we-the-audience are *disappointed* in the *failure*—for the sake of the *main character* and (sometimes) the world at large. Two stories that fall clearly into this category are *Chinatown* and *Butch Cassidy and the Sundance Kid*.

### Chinatown

In *Chinatown*, 1940s private detective Jake Gittes is hired by a woman who claims to be the wife of the Los Angeles Water Department chief engineer to spy on her husband because she suspects him of having an affair. When what appears to be proof of the affair is made public, the real wife appears and threatens to sue Jake for defamation. In pursuing the mystery of what instigated the fakery behind the first assignment, Jake discovers that the chief engineer has recently died in a suicide that smells like murder, and he sets his sights on discovering the truth behind the affair—to find out and expose to the world at large the identity of whoever committed the crime.

As I mentioned in Part One, any type of investigatory activity constitutes a *gain* action wherein the investigator seeks to *gain* (and usually make
public) the heretofore-unknown information that serves as the focus of the
investigation. Consequently, Jake is a *gain* character whose *course of action*
involves discovering the truth of what he believes to have been a crime. The
closer he gets to that truth, however, the more he suspects that the perpetrator may be a powerful figure who considers himself to be above the law.
This suspicion colors his *endeavor*, so that we may state the *proposition* as:

- One should *attempt* to discover (*gain* the identity of) and expose
  (*gain* the public knowledge of) the sins of those who think they
  are above the law, because *success in the attempt* will expose
  them to public scorn and uphold the idea that the law applies to
  all people equally regardless of their social class.

In *Chinatown*, Jake finds out who is responsible for murdering the chief
engineer and uncovers along the way a lot of disturbing information about
the depravity of the killer. But due to matters of money and power, Jake
*fails* to expose the responsible party and thereby bring him to justice. We-
the-audience want Jake to *succeed*, but he does not, and we are left *disappointed*. And because our hopes for his *success* are dashed at the end of his
journey, *Chinatown* stands as a prime case of a *fail/disappointed* story.

## Butch Cassidy and the Sundance Kid

In *Butch Cassidy and the Sundance Kid*, the *main character*, Butch, and
his buddy, Sundance, are a pair of likeable Old West bank robbers whose
careers go awry when they branch out into train robbery and decide to rob
the same train twice, thinking that the company that owns the train will not
expect the second try. Not only does the second robbery go wrong, but the
first one prompts the train company to hire a crack troop of freelance law-
men to hunt them down and kill them.

From that point forward, the story centers on their *attempt* to *keep* their
freedom in light of a threat to their lives. They employ various strategies to
do so, including fleeing their pursuers, seeking support from a girlfriend,
escaping to another country, and even going straight—none of which work.
And when they return to robbery as a way to make ends meet, they are
found out and forced into an ultimate confrontation.

Because Butch and Sundance are good-hearted, likeable men who do
not seek to cause intentional harm to other people, we-the-audience are apt
to hope for their *success* in *keeping* free from their pursuers—who represent
the long arm of a powerful corporation. In a philosophical sense, in fact,
their story represents the fight for freedom against control. And its *proposition* may be stated as:

- One should *attempt* to *keep* his freedom against the threat of its extinction, because *success in the attempt* will preserve the prospect of living a satisfying life.

which elevates their story of personal survival to one that affirms the value of freedom itself.

In a freeze frame that saves us from having to witness the complete annihilation of Butch and Sundance, the storytellers make clear that they do not survive. In other words, they *fail* to beat the forces of control, and we are left *disappointed* by their *failure*. As a result, *Butch Cassidy and the Sundance Kid* drops plainly into the *fail/disappointed* bin.

## CREATING AND USING AN OUTCOME/REACTION TABLE

To appreciate the usefulness of the *outcome/reaction* quartet, it is helpful to build a table that sorts stories into each of its four categories. Doing so is more than just an exercise in sorting; it generates a landscape that the writer can use to locate her story in the world of stories at large. And by comparing her story to those of a similar type, she may glean significant insights that apply to the type as a whole and employ them in the development of her own work.

If we include the stories that I have used as examples in this book, and throw in a few others to help broaden the range of those listed, our *outcome/reaction* table looks like this, where each listing includes the *type of intent* of the *main character.*[*]

| outcome | reaction | |
|---|---|---|
| | *pleased* | *disappointed* |
| succeed | – *Back to the Future* (*regain*) <br> – *Blade Runner* (*regain*) <br> – *Four Weddings and a Funeral* (*gain*) <br> – *The Fugitive* (*regain*) <br> – *Lord of the Rings* (*regain*) <br> – *Panic Room* (*keep*) <br> – *Rocky* (*gain*) <br> – *Whale Rider* (*gain*) <br> – *The Wizard of Oz* (*regain*) | – *The Player* (*keep*) <br> – *Swimming with Sharks* (*gain*) |

---

[*] To avail yourself of an ever-expanding collection of story analyses grouped in this manner, visit the *Soul of Your Story Academy* website at www.soulofyourstory.com.

| outcome | reaction | |
| --- | --- | --- |
| | *pleased* | *disappointed* |
| *fail* | – A Christmas Carol (*keep*) <br> – Big Night (*gain*) <br> – Casablanca (*keep*) <br> – How the Grinch Stole Christmas! (*gain*) <br> – The Piano (*keep*) | – Butch Cassidy and the Sundance Kid (*keep*) <br> – Chinatown (*gain*) <br> – Romeo and Juliet (*gain*) |

Even a cursory glance at the table reveals two significant insights: a) that *succeed/pleased* stories dominate the universe of produced and published works and b) that the *outcome/reaction* classification is independent of the *type of intent*. Both deserve a brief looking into.

## Dominance of Succeed/Pleased Stories

The dominance of *succeed/pleased* stories is not a result of any bias on my part. It stems, instead, from their tendency to conclude in crowd-pleasing endings. And although their marketability does not speak to their value as art (pro or con), it does effect their chances of being produced. Thus it has been for thousands of years, and thus it will be as long as human beings roam the planet.

By contrast, *succeed/disappointed* stories are rare, in part because they tend to leave the audience unnerved. It is troubling to see a sin go unpunished, even when confirming condemnation of the sin. Such stories tend to disturb us regardless of how well they are produced. And if we-the-audience are given a choice between satisfaction and agitation, most of us will opt for the former.

## Independence of the Type of Intent

In every quadrant of the table, we find a mix of *types of intent*. The list of *succeed/pleased* stories, for example, includes everything from *Rocky* (*gain*) to *Back to the Future* (*regain*) to *Panic Room* (*keep*).

It should come as no surprise that the *outcome* of a story is independent of its *type of intent*. After all, the *type of intent* defines our measure of progress in the story but does not speak to the advisability of the *endeavor*. And the matter of whether the *main character succeeds* is solely in the hands of the writer—depending on how she chooses to argue in support of the story *proposition*. Consequently, the *type of intent* and the *outcome* of the story are completely unrelated, and we should expect to see *types of intent* of all types in every quadrant of the table. Which we do.

## USING CONSOLATIONS AND COLLATERAL DAMAGE

As I noted when introducing the *outcome/reaction* quartet, the audience *reaction* does not determine its *mood*—that is, whether an ending is received as *happy* or *unhappy*. For example, in a story that involves an *advisable endeavor*, we-the-audience might be *pleased* with the *outcome* but *unhappy* at the end, because of the heavy price paid by the *main character* to *succeed*. Conversely, we might be *disappointed* with the *outcome* and yet *happy* at the end, owing to benefits that stem from his *failed attempt*.

The seeming disconnect between these classifications may be explained by looking at the fallout from the *attempt*—specifically, at the *consolations* (benefits) or *collateral damage* (injuries) that result from the effort involved. For example, if an out-of-shape housewife sets her sights on running a marathon, and changes her lifestyle in positive ways to do so, we-the-audience will root for her to *succeed* and reap *rewards* of her *success*. But even if she *fails* and is unable to finish the race, it is likely that she will benefit from the preparations themselves. She might, for example, improve her health or even make new friends. In any case, she profits simply by making the *attempt* and is rewarded with improvements to her life. The *outcome* of *failure disappoints* us, to be sure, but her positive *consolations* leave us *happy*.

Similarly, if our killer of aliens sends the invasion packing, we are likely to be *pleased* with the result. But the death of his lover is *collateral damage* he will suffer the rest of his life. The planet is saved (Huzzah!), and we are *pleased*, but our hero mourns his lover, which makes us *unhappy*.

By recognizing the roles of *consolations* and *collateral damage* in her story, the writer can free herself from the natural tendency to equate the words "*success*," "*pleased*," and "*happy*"—and their negative counterparts, "*failure*," "*displeased*," and "*unhappy*." The principles of *thematic imprinting* work like an acetylene torch, destroying the links between them.

# Chapter 11

## THE OTHER SHORT TOUR

Okay, let's take a breath... and another tour.

— ✆ ♦ ✆ —

Every great story contains at its heart a *theme* that serves as its artistic statement to the world. In a story, the *theme* takes the form of a *thematic declaration* expressed through the actions and behaviors of its characters and their effects on the *outcome* of the plot. The *thematic declaration* may be expressed by means of a *thematic grammar* constructed from rules and principles that intertwine directly with those of the *grok approach*.

An effective *thematic grammar* can be derived from the ancient roots of storytelling as a means of passing on and preserving cultural knowledge. Such knowledge usually takes the form of writ-large statements of advice regarding the proper way to live. If the advice is made personal, however, as it would be if shared between friends, it reveals itself to be intended not for the world at large but for the specific recipient of the story.

The advice can be stated simply as "You should" or "You should not" but may be refined for use as the basis of a *thematic grammar* consisting of three elements:

- *Proposition*
- *Outcome*
- *Reaction*

The *proposition* is the explicit assertion made by the story. The *outcome* is the result of an *attempted endeavor* related to the *proposition*. The *reaction* is the response elicited in the audience upon experiencing the revelation of the *outcome*. When properly combined, these elements work together to imprint the *theme* into the very fabric of the story—which is why the process of doing so may be referred to as "*thematic imprinting.*"

The *proposition* derives from the idea that the *theme* of a story may be thought of as a piece of advice offered from the writer to her audience. When broadly stated forms of such advice are made personal and specific, they result in a pair of generic *propositions* that can be written as:

- One should *attempt* to [*endeavor*], because *success in the attempt* [*reward of success*].

- One should not *attempt* to [*endeavor*], because *success in the attempt* [*harm of success*].

One or the other of these *propositions* (but not both at the same time) can be used to express the *theme* of any story.

At the heart of every *endeavor* lies an *issue* around which the story may be said to revolve. The *issue* may be thought of as the area of concern to be debated in the story, and the *theme* may be thought of as the opinion of the story on the *issue*.

The *issue* may be stated in general terms, such as "appreciating your blessings" or "taking revenge" but must manifest as a *course of action* and be refined by the motivation (*why*) and methods (*how*) that are used to transform the *course of action* into an *endeavor*. Every significant character in the story, including the *main character*, sheds the light of opinion on the *issue* from a unique perspective defined by his or her role in the story. Likewise, the *issue* serves as a point source of light that casts important and revealing shadows on each of the characters.

*Issues* can be derived from many sources, including matters of concern to the writer herself and published or produced works regarding human behavior, values, or morality. Regardless of the opinion contained in the source of the *issue*, the writer is free to use the *issue* however she likes so that her story presents her own viewpoint.

To identify the *issue* that lies at the heart of a story under development, the writer can look to the significant characters in the story and/or to the *inciting incident* that generates the *intent* of the *main character*. If the story springs spontaneously from the mind of the writer, each significant character will naturally manifest a relationship to the *issue* in his or her behaviors. And regardless of its location in the story, the *inciting incident* contains important clues regarding the *issue*.

The *outcome* expresses the *succeed*-or-*fail* result of the *attempt* by the *main character* to pursue the *endeavor* contained in the *proposition*. The *reaction* represents the expected audience response to the *outcome*. These two elements work together to render the *thematic declaration* of the story and thereby express the story *theme*. Due to the natures of the *outcome* and *reaction*, it is possible to classify any story as belonging to one of four types:

- *succeed/pleased*
- *succeed/disappointed*
- *fail/pleased*
- *fail/disappointed*

An examination of stories that see the light of publication or production reveals that most constitute *succeed/pleased* stories, wherein the *main character succeeds* in the *attempt* of an *advisable endeavor* and the audience is *pleased* at the *outcome*. Very few stories fit into the *succeed/disappointed* type, wherein the *main character succeeds* in the *attempt* of an *inadvisable endeavor*, and the audience feels *disappointed* with the *outcome*.

Although the audience *reaction* affects the *thematic declaration*, it does not determine its *mood*—that is, whether the ending is seen as *happy* or *unhappy*. That determination depends, in part, on any *consolation* or *collateral damage* that results from the *attempt*.

So now that we have explored the ins and outs of the *grok approach* (in Part One), learned the basic tenets of *thematic grammar*, and witnessed how both intertwine to create a unified approach to developing stories, only one matter remains to be explored—how to use this knowledge to create a new story from scratch, steer any story under development, and/or cut away the chaotic underbrush that threatens to choke or halt the progress of a story that is otherwise developing well.

In other words, it is time to introduce the idea of *meta-adaptation*.

# Part Three

## Meta-adaptation

# Chapter 12

## PRINCIPLES OF META-ADAPTATION

As I showed in Part Two, the principles of the *grok approach* are linked to those of *thematic imprinting* by a critical element that lies at the heart of each—the *intent* of the *main character*. It is this bond between the two techniques that allows them to be used in tandem to dig down into a story, revealing its soul. And it is the exposure of that soul, along with the knowledge of how to study it properly, that allows the writer to probe it for insights and express it most effectively in her story.

I refer to the practice of using the *grok approach* and *thematic imprinting* in this coordinated manner as "*meta-adaptation*," where the butt of the term (*adaptation*) stems from the idea that the writer can use the practice to adapt a story idea from any source, and the prefix (*meta*) represents the idea that the adaptation is executed from the inside—by probing the source to discover the features that lie behind its façade and using them to create the new story.

And although the practice of *meta-adaptation* is designed primarily to help the writer create and develop new stories, it can also be used to guide the growth of those already in development. How so? By providing her with an orderly course of questioning based on the *grok approach* and *thematic imprinting* and prompting her to steer its development along an organic path.

# Chapter 13

## PRACTICING META-ADAPTATION

It is important to note at the outset that *meta-adaptation* is not a single technique. It is, instead, an overall practice consisting of many techniques, each of which can be applied to the process of developing any story. Each technique may be thought of as a specialized tool, and the practice as a whole may be thought of not as the toolbox but as an apprenticeship that leads to their mastery.

Its exploration is best approached from two standpoints:

• General method
• Starting points

The general method defines the overall scheme for dissecting a story idea into its *grok*-related pieces, deriving insights from the pieces, and using the insights to create a new story or fix one in need of repair. It consists mainly of asking the questions that reveal the soul of the story. The starting points are specialized gates of entry for using the overall practice.

## GENERAL METHOD

Because *meta-adaptation* involves the coordinated use of the *grok approach* and *thematic imprinting*, both techniques must be accounted for in its general method. In describing the method, however, it is best to explore the aspects of each technique separately and to cross-reference them wherever necessary—which is what I will do here.

### ASPECTS DRAWN FROM THE *grok* APPROACH

The primary aspects of *meta-adaptation* that are drawn from the *grok approach* include:

• Identifying the *main character*
• Identifying the *intent* and *treasure*
• Examining the *treasure*
• Identifying and examining the *core ensemble*
• Exploring the *inciting incident*

## Identifying the Main Character

As should be clear by this point (unless you skipped to this page from the preface), the burden of telling in any story lies primarily with its *main character*, who constitutes the vehicle that we-the-audience climb inside to experience the world of the story and navigate its valleys and peaks. He generates the story by means of his *intent*, provides the standard of measure that we-the-audience use to determine story movement, and carries the story *theme*.

Because the *main character* shoulders the bulk of the workload in any story, his identification is critical to the *meta-adaptation* process. And the writer is well-advised to find him early on, so that other important aspects of the story can be made in his context. Some *meta-adaptation* starting points require his identification at the outset; others may defer the task. At some point in every case, however, he must be found and bestowed with a badge of honor befitting his position.

## Identifying the Intent and Treasure

It is not sufficient, of course, to merely identify the *main character*; the writer must also find his *intent* and *treasure*. And because the two share the same heart, they must be searched for as a set. Consequently, the process of finding them involves a simultaneous exploration for both according to the methods outlined in Chapter 6.

The *intent* and *treasure* are far more important to the development of a story than are illustrative details about the *main character* and his world. Although such details may enhance the story, they cannot on their own propel it or help craft it in significant ways. Simply put, detail without direction creates a purposeless junk yard of imagery, not a story.

## Examining the Treasure

As with many aspects of *meta-adaptation*, examining the *treasure* can be a trial-and-error process. Although an initial guess may prove wrong or incomplete, the mere act of conjecture can raise important questions that get the mental juices flowing and ultimately inform and enhance the story.

To examine completely the *treasure* for any *main character*, the writer must pose the full slate of questions relevant to its description—for example:

· Is the *treasure* plausible in the context of the story world?

· How does the *main character* come to possess it as the focus of his *intent?*

· Where is it located in the timeline of the story (past, present, or future)?

· Is it *objective* or *subjective? External* or *internal?*

· What *inner goal* does the *main character* pursue by *attempting* to accomplish the *outer goal* associated with it?

Each of these questions helps the writer to identify the *treasure* in its most potent form and to explore its relationship to the *main character* by whom it is possessed. By seeking their answers, the writer embarks on a meditative journey through the story and returns from the journey with insights that enrich the story with respect to both its inner construction and the details of its telling.

## Identifying and Examining the Core Ensemble

As I noted in Chapter 2, stories are usually populated by a multitude of characters, from those that serve as living props to those that are crucial to the telling. Regardless of its population, however, the story is primarily served by a *core ensemble* of characters, and it is out of this group that the *main character* steps forward to hoist the story onto his back. Although it is possible to create a story that involves only one character, most stories include a full-blown *core ensemble* whose job is not merely to keep the *main character* company but to occupy roles such as Ally, Conscience, Helper, or Hindrance. Such characters also help to shine important perspectives on the *issue* that lies at the heart of the story *theme*.

Because the *core ensemble* is vital to the story, the practice of *meta-adaptation* demands that it be identified and thoroughly examined. In particular, each of its members must be looked at in terms of his or her role in the journey of the *main character* and the perspective that he or she provides with respect to the story *issue*.

## Exploring the Inciting Incident

It goes nearly without saying that every story springs into existence by virtue of an *inciting incident*. At some point in the process of *meta-adaptation*, therefore, it is necessary to explore the *inciting incident*, not only with respect to its particulars but with regard to two of its most fundamental aspects:

· Placement in the timeline of the story
· Role in initiating the story and defining its *theme*

With regard to its placement in the timeline of the story, the *inciting incident* may occur in the first act or even before the story begins for us-the-audience. Regardless of where it occurs, however, it constitutes the key that starts the story engine. Its placement in the timeline affects only the manner in which it is revealed to us-the-audience. But since we-the-audience are those whom the writer seeks to engage, it behooves her to consider very carefully the effect of her choices when doing so.

In addition to launching the story, the *inciting incident* provides important clues regarding the *intent* of the *main character* and his role as its primary driver. Such clues may be found by viewing the *inciting incident* through the lenses of *why*, *how*, and *what*—for example:

- *Why* is the *main character* compelled to take up the mission that his journey entails? And why now?
- *How* does the *inciting incident* differ from similar incidents that might have occurred in the past but did not prompt action?
- *What* does the *inciting incident* reveal about the story world, the *main character* himself, and the relationship between the two?

The *inciting incident* also contains important clues regarding the *issue* at the core of the story *theme*. Consequently, its exploration is vital to a complete understanding of the story.

## ASPECTS DRAWN FROM THEMATIC IMPRINTING

The main aspects of *meta-adaptation* drawn from *thematic imprinting* include:

- Identifying the *issue*
- Constructing the *proposition*
- Specifying the *outcome* and *reaction*
- Considering *consolations* and *collateral damages*

## Identifying the Issue

The very idea of *thematic imprinting* is based on the notion that every story contains at its heart a message and that the message can be thought of in terms of a *thematic declaration*. The complete *thematic declaration* results from combining the three main elements of *thematic grammar* described in Chapter 9—*proposition*, *outcome*, and *reaction*.

Every *proposition* is based on an *endeavor* that serves as the expression of an *issue*. The *issue* may be thought of as the subject up for discussion in the story, and the *theme* of the story constitutes the opinion of the story concerning the *issue*.

Because the *issue* lies at the heart of the story *theme*, it must be searched for, identified, explored, and expressed in terms of a *grok type of intent*. This task may be accomplished, in part, by examining the *inciting incident* that prompts the *main character* to *attempt* her *endeavor* in the first place. And clues to the identity of the *issue* may also be found by examining each member of the *core ensemble* and looking for an *issue* that is of common concern to all.

## Constructing the Proposition

The *proposition* of any story is stated best in terms of an *attempted endeavor* on the part of the *main character*. Consequently, in *meta-adaptation*, the *issue* must be translated into an *endeavor*. *Meta-adaptation* also requires the writer to render a value judgment regarding whether the *endeavor* is *advisable* (recommended) or *inadvisable* (warned-against).

In addition to this value judgment, the *proposition* must address the prospective *consequence* of *success in the attempt* of the *endeavor*. For an *advisable endeavor*, such a *consequence* may be thought of as a *reward* to be reaped by *success in the attempt*. Conversely, for an *inadvisable endeavor*, it is a *harm* to be suffered—also from *success in the attempt*. In either case, the *consequence* hones the *proposition* and thereby refines the story *theme*.

Although the *consequence* of *success in the attempt* may follow naturally from matters surrounding the *issue*, the writer is free to specify it and to thereby define the stakes for the *main character*. She is also free to specify the *consequence* of *failure in the attempt*—and doing so may prove necessary to completely encompass the *goals* of the *main character*.

In either case, the *proposition* requires only the *consequence* (*reward* or *harm*) of *success*, not that of *failure*.

## Specifying the Outcome and Reaction

Although the *proposition* is a necessary element of the *thematic declaration*, it is not sufficient to express the story *theme*. It is merely the assertion that the writer proposes to defend by telling the story. To fully express the *theme* of the story, the writer must specify not only the *proposition* itself but the *outcome* of the *attempted endeavor* and the expected audience *reaction* upon learning the *outcome*.

In *thematic imprinting*, the *outcome* of the story is stated strictly in terms of the *success* or *failure* of an *attempt* by the *main character* to pursue a specific *endeavor*. Because the *outcome* is crucial to the argument put forth by the story, it must be clearly determined when developing the story and recognized for its role in expressing the *theme*.

The writer must also consider the expected audience *reaction* to the *outcome* (*pleased* or *disappointed*). In point of fact, it is the interaction of the *outcome* and *reaction* that creates the final conclusion supporting the *theme*. It is possible, for example, to support an *advisable endeavor* by portraying either a *successful attempt* that leaves us-the-audience *pleased* or a *failed attempt* that leaves us *disappointed*. Neither approach is superior to the other, and the writer is free to choose either, depending on how she prefers to express the story *theme*.

## Considering Consolations and Collateral Damages

Although it is true that the *outcome* and *reaction* combine to express the *theme* of the story, they do not by themselves determine its *mood*—that is, whether its ending renders the audience *happy* or *unhappy*. That determination is made, in part, by the *consolations* and *collateral damages* that result from the pursuit of the *endeavor*.

To develop a complete understanding of a story ending, including its *mood*, the *meta-adaptation* process requires the writer to examine the story in light of the possible *consolations* and *collateral damage* that accrue to the *main character* in his journey. Doing so not only helps her attain a thorough understanding of the story, it can lead to insights regarding its arc and even, in some cases, expose story paths that are more truthful than those she originally envisioned.

# STARTING POINTS

The power of *meta-adaptation* stems not only from its broad applicability but from its multitude of potential starting points. It can be used, for example, to generate stories from existing works of fiction or to derive them from news items, real-life persons, or matters of debate. Regardless of starting point, however, *meta-adaptation* creates an instructional roadmap for the development and realization of the resulting story.

Like any *grok*-related effort, *meta-adaptation* can sometimes involve a trial-and-error process whereby the writer makes an informed guess regarding the answer to a question, examines the answer in light of the *grok approach* and *thematic imprinting*, and refines the guess based on the results. In this regard, the practice of *meta-adaptation* may be said to serve as spirit guide to steer the writer toward the organic truth of her story.

This section describes a set of major starting points for story creation and outlines the line of questioning best suited to each case. When creating and developing the story, the writer must address all of the questions raised in the general method outlined above. The starting point affects primarily the overall sequence in which they are addressed.

With that said, the major *meta-adaptation* starting points are:

- Existing story
- *Main character*
- *Issue*
- *Inciting incident*
- Upshot
- Item of information
- Matter of debate

## STARTING WITH AN EXISTING STORY

Adaptation has been used for thousands of years to refresh and update existing stories in order to render them palatable to current audiences. Just as the modern Broadway musical *West Side Story* is an adaptation of *Romeo and Juliet* written by William Shakespeare circa 1593, so *Romeo and Juliet* may derive, in part, from a novel published by Masuccio Salernitano in 1476, which in turn contains elements that are present in the story of *Pyramus and Thisbe* published by the Roman poet Ovid in his work titled *Metamorphoses*.

In most adaptations, the names and story backdrops may change, but the characters, conflicts, and *core ensembles* remain pretty much the same. In *West Side Story*, for example, the setting of Verona, Italy, is replaced by New York City, Romeo and Juliet become Tony and Maria, and the warring Montague and Capulet families become rival street gangs, the Jets and the Sharks.

Each such adaptation represents what one might call a "surface adaptation"—that is, a recasting of the basic story with all of its external elements intact. The difference between surface adaptation and *meta-adaptation* lies largely in the ability of *meta-adaptation* to dig deep into the inner workings of the story that serves as the source—to expose its spine and soul and by doing so reveal the essential elements that can be used to create a new story from scratch. The external trappings of a story created by *meta-adaptation* may hardly resemble those of the story from which it was derived, but if the writer does her job well, the adaptation may be exact in the finest detail with respect to the souls of the two stories.

The process of using *meta-adaptation* to create a story based on an existing work of fiction involves two basic steps:

Step 1. Deconstructing the existing story

Step 2. Building the new story

The first step involves dissecting the existing work into its fundamental pieces, thereby exposing its true internal nature and construction. The second step uses those pieces to build a new work. The new work may differ in every external respect from the story on which it is based, but its internal nature will demonstrate clearly its inspiration.

## Step 1. Deconstructing the Existing Story

Because an existing story is fully expressed and populated with characters, its potential *meta-adaptation* starting points are legion. But before any of them can be used, the existing story must be deconstructed into its basic *grok approach* and *thematic imprinting* pieces. Although the deconstruction is not performed strictly step-by-step, it can be guided by the following set of questions (presented here in approximate order of importance).

- Who is the *main character*?
  - What is his *type of intent*?
  - What is his *treasure*? Is it *objective* or *subjective*, *external* or *internal*, *outer* or *inner*? Is it complete in itself, or is it merely a *trophy* of some deeper *treasure*? And if so, what is that deeper *treasure*?
- What is the *endeavor attempted* by the *main character*?
  - What is the *course of action* contained in the *endeavor*?
  - How do the *why* and *how* of the *attempt* affect the *endeavor*?
  - Is the *endeavor* presented as *advisable* or *inadvisable*?
- What is the *outcome* of the *attempted endeavor*?
- What is the expected audience *reaction* upon revelation of the *outcome*?
- What is the *issue* in the story?
  - How does the *issue* manifest in the *attempted endeavor*?
  - What is the opinion of the story regarding the *issue*?
- What is the fully stated story *proposition*?
- What is the *consequence* associated with *success in the attempt*?
  - Is the *consequence* a *reward* or *harm*? Is it presented as a *goal* to be sought or one to be feared?
  - Is the *consequence* of *failure in the attempt* made known?
  - How does it relate to any *consolations* or *collateral damage*?
- Which strategies and tactics does the *main character* use in the *attempt* to pursue his *endeavor*?
  - Which strategies and tactics *succeed* and which *fail*?
- Which characters comprise the *core ensemble*?
  - What role does each *core ensemble* member play with respect to the *main character* and his journey? Ally? Conscience? Opponent?
  - How does each *core ensemble* member relate to the *issue*?
- What is the *inciting incident* that starts the motor of the story?
  - Where is the *inciting incident* located in the storyline, and how is it conveyed to the audience?
- At what point is the audience made fully aware who the *main character* is, what he *intends*, and *why* he possesses the *intent*?

When employing such questions to probe and dissect the existing story, it is important to focus not only on the questions themselves but on the manner in which the story provides clues to their answers. That is to say, each of these questions merits a follow-up question: How is the answer made known?

## Step 2. Building the New Story

After the existing work of fiction has been deconstructed, the writer can use any or all of its internal elements as starting points for the creation of the new story. And she can do so simply by applying their *grok approach* and *thematic imprinting* characteristics to her new story world.

The disciplinarian outpost captain becomes the overprotective mother. The outpost perimeter becomes the familial boundaries. The seductive ease of the sweltering jungle becomes the tempting world of modern adolescent life. The mutinous brigade of outpost soldiers becomes a set of disgruntled siblings. And each group is led by a charismatic figure of revolution who *intends* to *gain* freedom for himself and his peers by forcing the hand of the oppressor while seeking a peaceful resolution—an *advisable endeavor*. Each renegade leader may call on allies, engage in acts of subterfuge, and fight the impulse to end the matter quickly with a devastating coup.

Regardless of which elements of the existing work are used to create the new story, any story created in this fashion represents an adaptation of the existing story at its most fundamental level. Which is what the practice of *meta-adaptation* is all about.

## STARTING WITH A MAIN CHARACTER

Using a *main character* as a starting point for *meta-adaptation* can prove advantageous to the writer, because the person on whom the *main character* is based, whether real or imagined, is likely to possess a set of traits that allow the writer to fictionalize him easily. Such traits might need to be reworked a bit as the story develops, but they can provide important clues to the answers that must be sought in the *meta-adaptation* process outlined above.

In general, *main characters* that can serve as *meta-adaptation* starting points are drawn from either of two sources:

+ Real persons

• Imagined persons

The real persons might be dead or living, extracted from the pages of history textbooks or from grocery-store checkout-line tabloids. The imagined persons might spring to life from what-if scenarios, such as, "What if a friendless adolescent girl were granted the magical gift of making anyone like her?"

Regardless of which type of person is used as a starting point, however, the main challenge for the writer is that of transforming the static image of the person into a dynamic *endeavor* that can drive effective action in the story. And the process of doing so varies slightly depending on whether the starting-point person is real or imagined.

## Main Characters Based on Real Persons

*Main characters* that are based on real persons may or may not represent the actual persons on whom they are based. The writer may use a "biopic" style that chronicles the life of the actual person or create a completely fictional *main character* whose nature, struggles, and/or accomplishments mirror those of the real person who serves as its source. Regardless of which approach is used, however, the principles of *meta-adaptation* help the writer to create a *main character* who reflects accurately the motivations that drive the real person in any episode or era of his life.

The process of using *meta-adaptation* to develop a story based on a real person involves the following steps (in recommended sequence).

Step 1. Identifying the *type of intent*

Step 2. Discovering the *treasure*

Step 3. Determining the *inciting incident*

Step 4. Building the *core ensemble*

Step 5. Investigating *strategies* and *tactics*

Step 6. Identifying and expressing the *theme*

### *Step 1. Identifying the Type of Intent*

When using a real person as the starting-point, the writer must first identify his *type of intent*—including both the characteristic *type of intent* that defines his general tendencies and the specific *type of intent* that will drive the story. Although all of us exhibit the entire spectrum of *types of intent* in our daily lives, each of us tends to favor one over the others when it comes to directing our efforts, especially in times of stress and change. This characteristic *type of intent* may vary with factors such as age, gender, or cultural background, but it must be searched for and identified in order to create a *main character* who represents accurately the person on whom he is based.

It is especially important to identify the characteristic *type of intent* when creating a story that involves a broad time span in the life of the real person. Because the characteristic *type of intent* is basic to his nature, it influences his fundamental approach to life and new situations and serves as the active backdrop for the story. Consequently, it influences the actions and decisions he is likely to make in any circumstance, regardless of his age or situation.

By contrast, a story that focuses only on one particular episode in the life of the person is likely to be defined by the nature of the episode itself rather than the characteristic *type of intent*. His characteristic *type of intent* will influence his behaviors, to be sure, but the story will be driven primarily by the demands of the episode, not those of his nature.

## Step 2. Discovering the Treasure

In the course of identifying the *type of intent* for the real person, the writer must also discover his true *treasure* and its traits—for example, whether it is *objective* or *subjective, external* or *internal, outer* or *inner,* and whether it stands on its own or serves as a *trophy* of some deeper need. And here again, she must consider the time span of the story—specifically whether it will start in one era of his life and end in another or its events will play out in the course of minutes, days, months, or years.

For any story that involves a cross-era time span in the life of the real person, the *treasure* is likely to represent the *goal* of some long-held *inner treasure*—for example, the need for acceptance in light of a rejection early in life. For a story that involves a stand-alone episode, on the other hand, the *treasure* is likely to be short-term and specific. Regardless of time span or its length, however, the *treasure* must be found and made clear, so that we-the-audience can use it to measure progress and follow along in the story as it plays out.

## Step 3. Determining the Inciting Incident

When using a real person as the basis of a story, the writer must explore the real-world environment of that person for events or circumstances from which an *inciting incident* could arise. The *inciting incident* might be based on an actual occurrence or on a speculative "what-if" scenario, but in either case, it must be plausible and easily understood by the audience in the context of the story.

As with the *type of intent* and *treasure*, the nature of the *inciting incident* depends, in part, on whether the story involves a broad time span in the life of the *main character*. For a story that does involve a broad time span, the *inciting incident* is likely to take the form of an event that implants in him an unquenchable desire—for example, the death of a beloved pet that instills in him a lifelong need to help animals. For a story that involves a stand-alone episode the *inciting incident* tends to generate an *intent* that is more specific and focused on short-term desires.

After determining the nature of the *inciting incident*, the writer must establish its location in the story—specifically, whether it takes place before the story opens or somewhere in Act I. If it takes place before the story opens, she must construct the first part of the story such that the *inciting incident* is revealed to the audience either subtly, as a trail of interesting crumbs, or boldly, through an explosive revelation at the end of the act. If it takes place within the first act itself, then Act I can be viewed as "the tale of how the *main character* comes to obtain his *intent*."

## Step 4. Building the Core Ensemble

When the items mentioned in the prior steps have been identified, discovered, and determined, the writer can turn her attentions to the *core ensemble* and the roles of its members in the story. The composition of the *core ensemble* depends, in part, on the nature of the *main character* and his *intent* and *treasure* but also depends, again, on the story time span. For a story with a broad time span, the *core ensemble* may shift in tag-team fashion as the story evolves. An ally to the *main character* early in the story, for example, might be replaced later on by a different character who serves a similar purpose. For stories that represent stand-alone episodes, the *core ensemble* tends to stay intact from beginning to end.

## Step 5. Investigating Strategies and Tactics

For a story based on a real person, the writer may look to the real-world actions on the part of the source for clues regarding which strategies and tactics the *main character* is likely to employ in any situation. The real-world actions may also indicate the viability of any given strategy or tactic and provide the writer with possible obstacles that the *main character* will need to overcome in pursuit of his *endeavor*.

## Step 6. Identifying and Expressing the Theme

To identify and express the *theme* of the story, the writer must use elements identified above—for example, the *intent* and *treasure* of the source—to develop an *attempted endeavor*. She must also take a definitive stand with respect to its *advisability*, identify the *issue* at the heart of the *proposition*, and determine the desired *outcome* and audience *reaction*. When performing such operations for a *main character* based on a real person, the *hows* and *whys* that transform the *course of action* into an *endeavor* should be consistent with the nature of the person on whom the story is based.

# Main Characters Based on Imagined Persons

The process of using *meta-adaptation* to develop a story based on an imagined person is similar to that used for a story based on a real person. It differs primarily in the order with which its procedures are carried out, specifically (in recommended sequence):

Step 1. Identifying the defining characteristic

Step 2. Determining the *intent* and *treasure*

Step 3. Converting the *course of action* to an *endeavor*

Step 4. Specifying the *inciting incident*

Step 5. Building the *core ensemble*

Step 6. Identifying and expressing the *theme*

## Step 1. Identifying the Defining Characteristic

When using an imagined person as the starting point for *meta-adaptation*, the main challenge for the writer involves converting the defining characteristics of the imagined person into an *intent, treasure*, and *endeavor*. To do so, the writer must first identify which characteristics most accurately define the imagined person and cause him to spring to life in her mind. Does he have psychic powers? Is he exceptionally shy, lustful, gregarious, kind, or good looking? Is he the reincarnation of a medieval knight, a hardworking college grad down on his luck, or the father of an autistic child? It is from defining characteristics such as these that the writer must select a single characteristic that defines him best. And it is from this characteristic that the remainder of the *meta-adaptation* process springs.

## Step 2. Determining the Intent and Treasure

To convert the defining characteristic of the *main character* to an *intent* and *treasure*, the writer must imagine a scenario in which the characteristic is challenged to come into play. In doing so, it is not sufficient merely to think of a circumstance in which the characteristic is displayed; the circumstance must confront the characteristic head on and test its mettle. Whether the psychic powers are put to the test to save the life of a loved one or the lust must be curbed to preserve a marriage, it is the challenge to the defining characteristic that creates the *intent* that drives the story and defines the *treasure*.

## Step 3. Converting the Course of Action to an Endeavor

When the *intent* and *treasure* are combined with other imagined traits of the *main character* that help to define the *hows* and *whys* of his *attempt*, they convert his *course of action* into an *endeavor*. Instead of merely seeking revenge, a chieftain becomes a man *attempting* to rouse his tribe to action. Instead of merely solving a scientific puzzle, a doctor becomes a woman *attempting* to cure her ailing child.

The *endeavor* that results from this conversion may be used directly as the basis of the *proposition* that defines the story *theme*.

## Step 4. Specifying the Inciting Incident

By imagining the scenario that challenges the defining characteristic of the *main character* (see above), the writer automatically generates the *inciting incident* for the story. Specifically, the *inciting incident* is the event or change in condition that prompts the challenge—for example, the kidnapping of the loved one that requires a man to test his psychic powers or the wifely ultimatum that challenges him to either curb his lust or risk losing the woman he loves.

After the *inciting incident* has been identified, the writer must determine where to place it in the timeline of the story. Doing so is a matter of story-telling preference and is unrelated to defining the story soul. The *inciting incident* sets things in motion, but nothing in its nature demands that it be located in a particular spot, as long as it occurs before the end of Act I.

## Step 5. Building the Core Ensemble

After the *endeavor* and *inciting incident* have been found, the writer must build the *core ensemble* of characters who either help or inhibit the *main character* in his journey. As I noted in Part Two, many clues regarding the *core ensemble* composition may be found in the *inciting incident* itself, and others may be gleaned from the nature of the challenge. Regardless of how the *core ensemble* is put together, however, the writer must expose its members, give them assignments, and place them where they belong in the story world.

## Step 6. Identifying and Expressing the Theme

When using an imagined person as a starting point for a story, most of the matters related to the *proposition* are determined early on—for example, in the finding of the *endeavor*. To fully express the *theme*, however, the *endeavor* must be judged as *advisable* or *inadvisable*, and the writer must determine the *outcome* and expected audience *reaction* upon its revelation. She must also identify any *consolations* or *collateral damage* that will influence the story *mood*—that is, whether it leaves the audience *happy* or *unhappy*.

And as with the placement of the *inciting incident*, she is free to specify such matters as she sees fit.

## STARTING WITH AN ISSUE

Because the *endeavor* represents the playing out of an *issue*, it is possible to use an *issue* itself as a starting point and to work backwards from there to flesh out the story details. The process of using an *issue* as the *meta-adaptation* starting point involves the following procedures (in recommended sequence).

Step 1. Developing the *endeavor*

Step 2. Creating the *proposition*

Step 3. Extracting the *main character*

Step 4. Building the new story

In this case, the *meta-adaptation* process is reversed from those that use either an existing story or a *main character* as their starting points, because the *endeavor* is developed prior to identification of the *main character*.

## Step 1. Developing the Endeavor

To transform an *issue* into an *endeavor*, the writer must transform the *issue* into a *course of action* and incorporate the *how* and *why* that converts the *course of action* to an *endeavor*. The *how* and *why* that she uses to do so depend, to some extent, on the particulars of the story to be created; however, it is entirely possible to propose first guesses for them and include one or both in the *proposition*.

For example, if we begin with the *issue* of "defying authority," we can convert it quite easily to an outward *course of action* as "committing a public act of defiance." If we then add a *why* of "to draw attention to a social injustice," we end up with an *endeavor* that can be expressed as, "commit a public act of defiance to draw attention to a social injustice."

## Step 2. Creating the Proposition

After the *endeavor* has been developed, it must be judged by the writer as *advisable* or *inadvisable* so that it can be couched properly in terms of a *proposition*. The *advisability* affects how the *proposition* is phrased and how the *outcome* and *reaction* are used to express the story *theme*.

To create the *proposition*, the writer must also determine the *type of intent* of the *endeavor* and the *consequence* of *success in the attempt*. The *endeavor* described above, for example, represents a *gain* action wherein the *reward* of *success in the attempt* might include the elimination of the exposed injustice—in which case the fully formed *proposition* could be expressed:

- One should *attempt* to commit public acts of defiance to draw attention to (*gain* public awareness of) social injustice, because *success in the attempt* will create the possibility that the injustice will be exposed and eliminated.

This *proposition* defines the *type of intent* for the *main character* and sets the stage for determining the *outcome* and audience *reaction* that will work together to express the story *theme*.

## Step 3. Extracting the Main Character

When the *proposition* is fully expressed, it can be used to identify candidates for the role of *main character* in the story. The choice of *main character* plays a very large part in determining the particulars of the story. For example, a story involving a pay-it-forward action on the part of a wealthy old philanthropist differs greatly in its particulars from one involving a similar action on the part of a poor, crippled child. The two stories may differ, for example, with respect to their settings and *treasures*, but if both are constructed from the same *proposition*, they will share the same overall direction and story soul, including the *type of intent* of the *main character*.

## Step 4. Building the New Story

After the *main character* has been extracted from the *proposition*, the writer can begin to build the remainder of the story by identifying the *inciting incident*, putting together the *core ensemble*, and expressing the story *theme*. In this case, the details of the *inciting incident* and *core ensemble* help ground the story and render it tangible and worthy of poetic faith. The *theme*, as always, is expressed by means of its *outcome* and the audience *reaction*.

### Identifying the Inciting Incident

In any story, the *inciting incident* contains clues regarding the *issue*—and vice versa. When using an *issue* as a starting point, therefore, the *issue* itself may be used to identify the *inciting incident*. Specifically, the *inciting incident* should bring the *issue* to the attention of both the audience and the *main character*, thereby integrating it fully into the story and throughline of the *main character*.

### Building the Core Ensemble

When using an *issue* as a starting point, the writer is greatly aided in her ability to construct the *core ensemble*, because each of its members represents the light of an individual perspective on the *issue*. As a result, each member can be sought out, identified, and developed (in part) based strictly on his position on the *issue* as well as his or her function in the journey of the *main character*.

### Expressing the Story Theme

To fully express the *theme* of the story, the writer must determine not only the *endeavor* and its *consequence* of *success* but the *outcome* and audience *reaction*—both of which depend, in part, on whether the *endeavor* is *advisable* or *inadvisable*. The *thematic* argument of any story can be supported by either *success* or *failure* on the part of the *main character*, but the combined choice of *outcome* and *reaction* determine how the argument is made and received.

## STARTING WITH AN INCITING INCIDENT

*Inciting incidents* are well-suited as starting points for *meta-adaptation*, because each contains the core elements of a story, including likely candidates for the *main character* and *core ensemble* and the *issue* at the center of the *theme*. The candidates for *main character* and *core ensemble* typically constitute those who are most profoundly affected by the *inciting incident*, and the *issue* may be drawn from the circumstances surrounding its occurrence.

The process of using an *inciting incident* as the starting point involves the following procedures (in recommended sequence).

Step 1. Identifying the *main character*

Step 2. Discovering the *treasure*

Step 3. Exploring the *core ensemble*

Step 4. Finding the *issue*

Step 5. Building the story

# Step 1. Identifying the Main Character

To serve as the basis of a story, the *inciting incident* must be humanized so that its circumstances and ramifications draw the audience into the story and hold its attention. The first step toward doing so involves the identification of the *main character*.

Each of the characters whom the *inciting incident* affects may constitute a viable candidate for the role of *main character*, but only one of them may occupy the role in the story. In most cases, the best candidate is the character who is most affected by the *inciting incident*. For an *inciting incident* that affects an entire community—for example, the landing of an alien spacecraft in broad daylight on a busy city street—the best choice for *main character* is often a character for whom the event represents an upheaval of an otherwise mundane existence. Such a character represents an Everyman figure who is easily sympathized with by the audience.

# Step 2. Discovering the Treasure

After the *main character* is identified, the writer must probe the *inciting incident* with respect to its impact on his world and discover the specific *treasure* that is generated in its wake. The *treasure* determines the *type of intent* for the *main character*, and the *type of intent* can be used when formulating the *endeavor* that lies at the core of the *theme*.

# Step 3. Exploring the Core Ensemble

When the *main character* and *treasure* have been identified, the writer can turn her attention to identifying the *core ensemble*. Some of the *core ensemble* members may be drawn from characters who are directly affected by the *inciting incident*, but others merely gravitate toward the *main character* in his journey like iron filings attracted to a magnet. Regardless of his or her source of origin, each member of the *core ensemble* should aid or inhibit the *main character* in his journey through the story and should reflect the light of a unique perspective on the story *issue*.

## Step 4. Finding the Issue

As I noted above, the *inciting incident* in any story is directly related to the *issue*. Whether the *issue* involves finding lost love, ignoring the needs of others, or seeking forgiveness, the clues to its proper statement are contained in the *inciting incident*. To fully utilize the *issue* in the story, however, it must be used as the basis for an *endeavor* that, in turn, is used to create a *proposition*. In this manner, the story and its *theme* may be said to grow organically out of the *inciting incident*.

## Step 5. Building the Story

After the items listed above have been identified or determined, the writer may use them to build the remainder of the story, including its *proposition*, *theme*, *outcome*, and *reaction*. The specific methods for doing so are described elsewhere in this chapter and are based on the principles outlined in Chapter 10.

### STARTING WITH AN UPSHOT

Because the *grok approach* and *thematic imprinting* are integrated fully with respect to their roles in the development and telling of a story, it is possible to create a story designed to express an upshot—for example, a particular feeling or hoped-for *outcome*. For example, one can use *meta-adaptation* to create a story in which integrity triumphs over falsehood, perseverance leads to reward, or the common man wins out over the heartless machinations of a faceless authoritarian regime.

To use an upshot as the starting point for a story, the writer must translate it into an *issue* and use the techniques described above to develop the complete story based on the *issue*. When doing so, however, the writer is greatly aided with respect to her decisions regarding the *outcome* and expected *reaction* for the story. For example, if the upshot involves rewarding perseverance, it is likely that the *outcome* will involve *success in the attempt* for a *main character* whose *endeavor* requires perseverance—and that the writer will construct the story such that she expects the audience to be *pleased* with the *outcome*.

### STARTING WITH AN ITEM OF INFORMATION

*Meta-adaptation* can be used to create a story from nearly any item of information, whether it takes the form of juicy gossip overheard in a cafeteria or a scientific white paper. Because the spectrum of items that can be used in this regard is virtually limitless, it is not possible to construct a universal step-by-step procedure for applying *meta-adaptation* in every case.

In general terms, however, the item of information must be examined with respect to the characteristic that makes it newsworthy, and that characteristic must be used to provide clues regarding the best starting point for the *meta-adaptation* process. A face-in-the-news item, for example, might prompt a *meta-adaptation* that uses a *main character* based on a real person. An event-related item, on the other hand, might suggest the use of an *inciting incident*.

Regardless of which type of starting point is appropriate to the item, the process of story creation requires its expansion to include a *main character, treasure, type of intent, inciting incident, core ensemble,* and all of the *thematic* elements described elsewhere in this chapter.

## STARTING WITH A MATTER OF DEBATE

In addition to using concrete starting points, such as *main characters* and *inciting incidents*, the practice of *meta-adaptation* can be based on a matters of debate—for example, love versus hate, tradition versus modernity, or authority versus freedom. To use a matter of debate as the starting point for *meta-adaptation*, it must first be translated into an *issue*, such as "loving those who hate you" or "tearing down the old to erect the new." When the *issue* has been identified and clarified, the writer can use it to form an *endeavor*, establish the position of the story regarding the *advisability* of the *endeavor*, construct a fully formed *proposition*, and use the *proposition* to create the story according to the procedures outline above.

As with any *meta-adaptation* effort, however, the primary goal of the process involves humanizing the matter of debate by assigning it to a *main character* with a specific *type of intent* and *treasure* and using the story *outcome* and audience *reaction* to express the story *theme*. In the absence of a *main character* and the *grok approach* and *thematic imprinting* elements of his journey, the matter of debate constitutes nothing more than a strongly held position statement.

And the world is overrun with those already.

# Chapter 14

## THE LITTLEST TOUR

Because *meta-adaptation* may be thought of as the tunnel of love where the *grok approach* and *thematic imprinting* meet in the dark and pitch woo, it deserves its own little tour.

And this is it.

The principles of the *grok approach* are linked to those of *thematic imprinting* by a critical element that lies at the heart of each—that is, the *intent* of the *main character*. This element allows them to be used in tandem to discover and express the soul of any story and to develop new stories from scratch. The practice of doing so is referred to as "*meta-adaptation*," which works by providing the writer with an orderly course of questioning that allows her to analyze the hidden aspects of her story and develop it along its most organic path.

The practice of *meta-adaptation* may be approached in terms of a general method and set of basic starting points. The general method includes aspects drawn from both the *grok approach* and *thematic imprinting*, including (for the *grok approach*):

· Identifying the *main character*
· Identifying the *intent* and *treasure*
· Examining the *treasure*
· Identifying the *core ensemble*
· Exploring the *inciting incident*

and (for *thematic imprinting*):

· Identifying the *issue*
· Constructing the *proposition*
· Specifying the *outcome* and *reaction*
· Considering *consolations* and *collateral damages*

Each basic starting point may be thought of as a gateway through which *meta-adaptation* can be used to develop new stories. A basic (and non-exhaustive) set of such starting points includes:

- Existing story
- *Main character*
- *Issue*
- *Inciting incident*
- Upshot
- Item of information
- Matter of debate

The sequence in which the principles of the *grok approach* and *thematic imprinting* are applied in each case varies according to starting point. For some starting points, the *main character* and his *intent* and *treasure* are identified early on in the process. For others, the *intent* and *treasure* derive from an exploration of the *issue* or *inciting incident*. Regardless of the order in which the principles are applied, however, *meta-adaptation* allows them to be used in a coordinated manner to generate new stories from scratch.

And there you have it—the complete integration of the *grok approach* and *thematic imprinting* to create the practice of *meta-adaptation*... summarized in less than two pages.

It's time to go to storytelling town.[*]

---

[*] For details on how to get to storytelling town, where to stay, and how to get the most from your visit, see "Appendix A: Soul of Your Story Academy".

# Appendices

# Appendix A

## SOUL OF YOUR STORY ACADEMY

When you finished reading Part Three of this book, you might have thought you had reached the end. You had not.

You had, in fact, reached the beginning.

For although this book contains everything you need to know to understand and use the principles described in its pages, it simply cannot address the myriad of applications to which those principles apply. To do so would require a magical book—one capable of expanding overnight while you slept or during the day while you were at work, its pages filling with a burgeoning library of fresh examples of the *grok approach*, *thematic imprinting*, and *meta-adaptation* in action. A book in which you could jot questions in the margins and see the answers appear miraculously before you... and also see the questions other readers had asked and the answers that resulted from their queries. A book that served as a living codex of its principles and provided its readers with a channel of direct and ongoing contact with its author.

Or perhaps instead of a magical book, a website. An Internet haven where you could participate in the ongoing study, application, and development of the principles described in this book. An online sanctuary dedicated to story creation in the context of those principles and containing an ever-increasing knowledge base to help you learn to apply them.

Well, there is such a place. It's called the *Soul of Your Story Academy*, and its address is: www.soulofyourstory.com.

I'll meet you there.

# Appendix B

Throughout this book, I use certain words and phrases that are specific to the principles of the *grok approach* and *thematic imprinting*—for example, *type of intent* or *endeavor*. To provide helpful cues to the reader, I italicize such words wherever they are referenced.

This glossary includes brief, illustrative definitions for the words and phrases that are most fundamental to an understanding of the *grok approach* and *thematic imprinting*.

### attempt

Effort expended to achieve a *goal*. The presence or absence of *attempt* determines whether a *course of action* is driven by *intent* and is therefore suitable for use in a *proposition*.

### collateral damage

Injurious side effect that results from the *attempt* of an *endeavor*. If a hero saves the Earth from alien attack but suffers the loss of his family in the process, he is subject to the *collateral damage* of his *attempted endeavor*.

### consequence

Result of an *attempted course of action*. In a *proposition*, the *consequence* is expressed in terms of *rewards* or *harms* resulting from *success in the attempt*.

### consolation

Beneficial side effect that results from the *attempt* of an *endeavor*. If a character trains to run a race and loses the race but ends up healthier for her efforts, the physical fitness is a *consolation* of her *attempted endeavor*.

### core ensemble

Group of characters who are most actively involved in the story. The *main character* is the primary member of the *core ensemble*.

### course of action

Matter of doing that serves as the core of an *endeavor* expressed in a *proposition*—for example, "disrespecting power" or "investigating a crime."

### endeavor

Central element of a *proposition*. An *endeavor* expands the *course of action* to include the *why* and *how* of the *attempt*.

### fail/ disappointed

One of four possible combinations in the *outcome/ reaction quartet*. In a *fail/ disappointed* story, the *main character fails* in his *attempted endeavor*, and the audience is *disappointed* by the *outcome*.

### fail/ pleased

One of four possible combinations in the *outcome/ reaction quartet*. In a *fail/ pleased* story, the *main character fails* in his *attempted endeavor*, and the audience is *pleased* by the *outcome*—for example, because the *endeavor* is portrayed as detrimental to the *main character* or others in his world.

### failure

One of two possible *outcomes* for any *endeavor* (the other being *success*). Either *outcome* may be used by the writer to express a *thematic declaration* for the story.

### gain

One of three possible *types of intent* that describes the thrust of efforts for the *main character*. A *gain* character *attempts* to obtain a *treasure* that he has never before possessed.

### goal

Measurable objective pursued by the *main character*. The *goal* is expressed as a *treasure* to be *gained, regained,* or *kept*.

### grok

Acronym that describes the three possible *types of intent* for any character: to *gain* a *treasure* that he has never before possessed, to *regain* a *treasure* that he possessed previously and lost, or to *keep* a *treasure* that he currently possesses but is under threat of losing.

### grok approach

Consideration of a story in terms of its *main character* and his *attempt* to *gain, regain,* or *keep* a *treasure*. Stated broadly, such consideration consists of identifying the *intent* and *treasure* and exploring the implications of both on all other aspects of the story, including its *theme*.

## harm of failure

Injurious consequences of *failure* in an *attempted endeavor*. For example, the police detective who *fails* to identify and apprehend a serial killer leaves the killer free to kill again, which constitutes the *harm of failure* for the *endeavor*.

## harm of success

Injurious consequences of *success in the attempt* of any *endeavor*. For example, if a mother *attempts* to ignore the conflicts that brew within her family, then *success in the attempt* might cause the conflicts to fester until they explode, leaving the family in shambles.

## inciting incident

Event or circumstance that creates the impetus for the existence of the story. The *inciting incident* starts the motor of the story, usually by imparting to the *main character* the *intent* that motivates him and provides the spine of the story.

## intent

Purposeful action on the part of a character to achieve a *goal* and thereby satisfy a fundamental *want*. The *want* may provide the impetus for the *intent*, but it is the *intent* that drives the story movement.

## issue

Topic of concern regarding how to live that lies at the heart of the *proposition* and therefore stands at the core of the story *theme*. All characters and incidents in a fully integrated story cast light on its *issue* and thereby serve as arguments for and against its *thematic statement*.

## keep

One of three possible *types of intent* that describes the thrust of efforts for the *main character*. A *keep* character *attempts* to maintain possession of a *treasure* that is under threat of being lost.

## main character

Character around whom the story is constructed. The *main character* serves as the vehicle through which the audience experiences the story, generates the story by means of her *intent*, serves as an indicator of progress in the story, and bears the story *theme*.

## meta-adaptation

Process of combining the principles and practices of the *grok approach* and *thematic imprinting* to create entirely new stories based on existing works or on individual starting elements, such as characters or matters suggested by news items and articles.

## outcome

Ultimate judgment of the *attempt* of the *main character* as either *success* or *failure*. The *outcome* works in conjunction with the audience *reaction* to convey the story *theme*.

## outcome/reaction quartet

Group of four possibilities for the combination of story *outcome* and audience *reaction* for any story—*succeed/pleased*, *succeed/disappointed*, *fail/pleased*, and *fail/disappointed*. These four combinations may be used to define the manner in which the writer conveys the *theme* of any story.

## proposition

Definitive thematic statement that the writer asserts to be true and explores by means of the story—for example, that it is good for one to embrace change when the need or opportunity to do so arises. The writer supports the *proposition* through the story elements, as well as its ultimate *outcome* and *reaction*.

## rationale

Reasoning that serves as the basis for advice. The *rationale* typically appeals to the well-being of the advice recipient.

## reaction

Expected audience response to the *outcome* of the story, which can be expressed as either of two possibilities—*pleased* or *disappointed*. If the *outcome* matches the hopes of us-the-audience, given our sympathies and opinions regarding the *main character* and her *intent*, we will be *pleased*. If not, we will be *disappointed*.

## regain

One of three possible *types of intent* that describes the thrust of efforts for the *main character*. A *regain* character *attempts* to reacquire a *treasure* that he possessed previously but lost.

## reward of failure

Beneficial consequences of *failure* in an *attempted endeavor*. For example, if a staunch conformist whose orthodoxy is threatened *fails* in his *attempt* to *keep* a closed-minded world view and becomes more tolerant of others in the process, the new open-mindedness is his *reward of failure*.

## reward of success

Beneficial consequences of *success in the attempt* of any *endeavor*. For example, if a shipwrecked traveler *succeeds* in her *attempts* to return to civilization, the benefits of her reappearance in the civilized world constitute her *reward of success*.

## succeed/disappointed

One of four possible combinations in the *outcome/reaction quartet*. In a *succeed/disappointed* story, the *main character succeeds* in his *attempted endeavor*, and the audience is *disappointed* by the *outcome*, usually due to its *harm of success*.

## succeed/pleased

One of four possible combinations in the *outcome/reaction quartet*. In a *succeed/pleased* story, the *main character succeeds* in his *attempted endeavor*, and the audience is *pleased* by the *outcome*—for example, because she achieves an unselfish *goal* that benefits others as well as herself.

## success

One of two possible *outcomes* for any *endeavor* (the other being *failure*). Either *outcome* may be used by the writer to express a *thematic declaration* for the story.

## thematic declaration

Thematic statement asserted as true by the writer. The story itself lays out the case for and against the statement by means of its characters, events, *outcome*, and *reaction* and puts forth arguments in favor of the statement.

## thematic grammar

Consistent means of expressing the *theme* of any story, regardless of its medium, genre, type, or form. *Thematic grammar* consists of three primary elements—*proposition*, *outcome*, and *reaction*.

## thematic imprinting

Application of the principles of *thematic grammar* to express the story *theme*. *Thematic imprinting* works in conjunction with the *grok approach* and can be used, via the principles of *meta-adaptation*, to develop *themes* in stories adapted from existing works or other sources.

*theme*

Statement expressed by the story regarding how to live. The *theme* speaks to the audience member individually, rather than existing as a writ-large pronouncement.

*treasure*

Item or state of affairs that is considered to be valuable by the *main character*. The *treasure* provides the audience with a marker to determine story progress and the means to understand the ultimate *goal* of the *attempted endeavor* that provides the driving force for the story.

*type of intent*

One of three possible directions for the *intent* of any character: to *gain* a *treasure* that he has never possessed; to *regain* a *treasure* that he possessed previously; or to *keep* a *treasure* that he currently possesses. The *type of intent* of the *main character* determines the overall nature of the story.

*want*

Desire that serves as the impetus for an *intent*. A *want* is not sufficient by itself to generate story movement but provides the potential energy by which the *intent* can manifest as an *intended* action.

# Appendix C

Throughout this book, I use existing stories to illustrate the principles of the *grok approach* and *thematic imprinting*. Some are explored in depth; others are merely mentioned as examples of a kind. Most of them are reasonably well-known and demonstrate the principles at work in successful stories.

Although a few of the stories I mention exist as books or plays, most are films—which I prefer to refer to when teaching or writing about the *grok approach* and *thematic imprinting*, because they are easily accessible, can be experienced in their entirety in a relatively short period of time, and are typically based on a standard three-act story structure.

The following "story-ography" lists all of the books, plays, and films referred to in this book. Even without knowledge of or reference to the *grok approach* and *thematic imprinting*, it makes for some marvelous viewing and reading.

| Title | Details |
| --- | --- |
| *A Christmas Carol* | Medium: Novella (© 1843)<br> Multiple film adaptations from 1935<br>Author(s): Charles Dickens (1812-1870) |
| *Babe* (1995) | Medium: Film<br>Writer(s): George Miller, Chris Noonan<br>Director(s): Chris Noonan<br>Production Co.(s): Kennedy Miller Productions; Universal Pictures Entertainment<br>Adapted from: *The Sheep Pig* (Novel, © 1983) by Dick King-Smith |
| *Back to the Future* (1985) | Medium: Film<br>Writer(s): Robert Zemeckis, Bob Gale<br>Director(s): Robert Zemeckis<br>Production Co.(s): Universal Pictures; Amblin Entertainment |

| *Title* | *Details* |
|---|---|
| *Batman Forever* (1995) | Medium: Film<br>Writer(s): Bob Kane, Lee Batchler, Janet Scott Batchler, Akiva Goldsman<br>Director(s): Joel Schumacher<br>Production Co.(s): Warner Bros. Pictures; PolyGram Filmed Entertainment |
| *Big Night* (1996) | Medium: Film<br>Writer(s): Stanley Tucci, Joseph Tropiano<br>Director(s): Campbell Scott, Stanley Tucci<br>Production Co.(s): Rysher Entertainment; Timpano Production |
| *Blade Runner* (1982) | Medium: Film<br>Writer(s): Hampton Fancher, David Peoples<br>Director(s): Ridley Scott<br>Production Co.(s): The Ladd Company; Shaw Brothers; Warner Bros. Pictures; Michael Deeley Production; Ridley Scott Productions<br>Adapted from: *Do Androids Dream of Electric Sheep?* (Novel, © 1968) by Philip K. Dick |
| *Butch Cassidy and the Sundance Kid* (1969) | Medium: Film<br>Writer(s): William Goldman<br>Director(s): George Roy Hill<br>Production Co.(s): Twentieth Century Fox Film Corporation; Campanile Productions; Newman-Foreman Company |
| *Casablanca* (1942) | Medium: Film<br>Writer(s): Julius J. Epstein, Philip G. Epstein, Howard Koch<br>Director(s): Michael Curtiz<br>Production Co.(s): Warner Bros. Pictures<br>Adapted from: *Everybody Goes to Rick's* (Play, Unpublished © 1940) by Murray Burnett, and Joan Alison |
| *Chinatown* (1974) | Medium: Film<br>Writer(s): Robert Towne<br>Director(s): Roman Polanski<br>Production Co.(s): Paramount Pictures; Penthouse; Long Road Productions |

| Title | Details |
|---|---|
| *Four Weddings and a Funeral* (1994) | Medium: Film<br>Writer(s): Richard Curtis<br>Director(s): Mike Newell<br>Production Co.(s): PolyGram Filmed Entertainment; Channel Four Films; Working Title Films |
| *The Fugitive* (1993) | Medium: Film<br>Writer(s): Jeb Stuart, David Twohy<br>Director(s): Andrew Davis<br>Production Co.(s): Warner Bros. Pictures |
| *Harry Potter and the Sorcerer's Stone* (2001) | Medium: Film<br>Writer(s): Steve Kloves<br>Director(s): Chris Columbus<br>Production Co.(s): Warner Bros. Pictures; Heyday Films; 1492 Pictures<br>Adapted from: *Harry Potter and the Sorcerer's Stone* (Novel, © 1997) by J.K. Rowling |
| *How the Grinch Stole Christmas!* (1966) | Medium: Television (animated short special)<br>Writer(s): Dr. Seuss, Irv Spector, Bob Ogle<br>Director(s): Chuck Jones, Ben Washam<br>Production Co.(s): The Cat in the Hat Productions, MGM Television<br>Adapted from: *How the Grinch Stole Christmas!* (©1957) by Theodor Seuss Geisel, a.k.a. Dr. Seuss (1904–1991) |
| *The Lord of the Rings: Fellowship of the Ring* (2001) | Medium: Film<br>Writer(s): Fran Walsh, Philippa Boyens, Peter Jackson<br>Director(s): Peter Jackson<br>Production Co.(s): New Line Cinema; WingNut Films; The Saul Zaentz Company<br>Adapted from: *The Lord of the Rings: Fellowship of the Ring* (Novel, © 1954) by J.R.R. Tolkien |
| *Mad Max* (1979) | Medium: Film<br>Writer(s): James McCausland, George Miller<br>Director(s): George Miller<br>Production Co.(s): Kennedy Miller Productions; Crossroads; Mad Max Films |
| *The Odyssey* | Medium: Greek epic poem<br>Writer(s): Homer (ca. 8$^{th}$ century B.C.E.) |

| Title | Details |
| --- | --- |
| *Panic Room* (2002) | Medium: Film<br>Writer(s): David Koepp<br>Director(s): David Fincher<br>Production Co.(s): Columbia Pictures<br>   Corporation; Hofflund/Polone; Indelible<br>   Pictures |
| *The Piano* (1993) | Medium: Film<br>Writer(s): Jane Campion<br>Director(s): Jane Campion<br>Production Co.(s): The Australian Film<br>   Commission; CiBy 2000; Jan Chapman<br>   Productions |
| *The Player* (1992) | Medium: Film<br>Writer(s): Michael Tolkin<br>Director(s): Robert Altman<br>Production Co.(s): Avenue Pictures Productions;<br>   Spelling Entertainment; Addis Wechsler<br>   Pictures<br>Adapted from: *The Player* (Novel © 1988) by<br>   Michael Tolkin |
| *Rocky* (1976) | Medium: Film<br>Writer(s): Sylvester Stallone<br>Director(s): John G. Avildsen<br>Production Co.(s): Chartoff-Winkler<br>   Productions; United Artists |
| *Romeo and Juliet* (1968) | Medium: Film<br>Writer(s): William Shakespeare, Franco Brusati,<br>   Masolino D'Amico, Franco Zeffirelli<br>Director(s): Franco Zeffirelli<br>Production Co.(s): BHE Films; Verona<br>   Produzione; Dino de Laurentiis<br>   Cinematografica<br>Adapted from: *Romeo and Juliet* (Play) by<br>   William Shakespeare (1564–1616) |
| *Swimming with Sharks* (1994) | Medium: Film<br>Writer(s): George Huang<br>Director(s): George Huang<br>Production Co.(s): Cineville; Keystone Studios;<br>   Mama'Z Boy Entertainment |

| Title | Details |
| --- | --- |
| *Wall Street* (1987) | Medium: Film<br>Writer(s): Stanley Weiser, Oliver Stone<br>Director(s): Oliver Stone<br>Production Co.(s): Twentieth Century Fox Film<br>  Corporation; American Entertainment Partners<br>  L.P.; Amercent Films |
| *West Side Story* (1961) | Medium: Film<br>Writer(s): Ernest Lehman<br>Director(s): Jerome Robbins, Robert Wise<br>Production Co.(s): The Mirisch Corporation;<br>  Seven Arts Productions; Beta Productions<br>Based on the musical play *West Side Story* (1957),<br>  book by Arthur Laurents, music by Leonard<br>  Bernstein, lyrics by Stephen Sondheim |
| *Whale Rider* (2002) | Medium: Film<br>Writer(s): Niki Caro, Witi Ihimaera<br>Director(s): Niki Caro<br>Production Co.(s): South Pacific Pictures;<br>  ApolloMedia; Pandora Filmproduktion<br>Adapted from: *Whale Rider* (Novel, © 1987) by<br>  Witi Ihimaera |
| *The Wizard of Oz* (1939) | Medium: Film<br>Writer(s): Noel Langley, Florence Ryerson,<br>  Edgar Allan Woolf<br>Director(s): Victor Fleming<br>Production Co.(s): Metro-Goldwyn-Mayer<br>  (MGM); Loew's<br>Adapted from: The Wonderful Wizard of Oz by<br>  L. Frank Baum, illustrated by W. W. Denslow<br>  (©1900) |

# INDEX